SORCERER

'The only safe thing, my lord,'
he said in a clear, firm voice, 'is to kill them.
Witch. Devil's boy. Dog. The whole brood.
They have done their work here.
It cannot be undone.
But it can be revenged.'

Christopher Russell was a postman when he had his first radio play broadcast in 1975, having given up a job in the Civil Service to do shift work and have more daytime hours for writing. Since 1980, he has been a full-time scriptwriter and has worked on numerous television and radio programmes. Christopher lives with his wife on the Isle of Wight.

Books by Christopher Russell

Brind and the Dogs of War
Plague Sorcerer

CHRISTOPHER RUSSELL

PLAGUE SORCERER

PUFFIN

PUFFIN BOOKS

Published by the Penguin Group
Penguin Books Ltd, 80 Strand, London WC2R ORL, England
Penguin Group (USA) Inc., 375 Hudson Street, New York, New York 10014, USA
Penguin Group (Canada), 90 Eglinton Avenue East, Suite 700, Toronto, Ontario, Canada M4P 2Y3
(a division of Pearson Penguin Canada Inc.)
Penguin Ireland, 25 St Stephen's Green, Dublin 2, Ireland (a division of Penguin Books Ltd)
Penguin Group (Australia), 250 Camberwell Road, Camberwell, Victoria 3124, Australia
(a division of Pearson Australia Group Pty Ltd)
Penguin Books India Pvt Ltd, 11 Community Centre, Panchsheel Park, New Delhi – 110 017, India
Penguin Group (NZ), cnr Airborne and Rosedale Roads, Albany, Auckland 1310, New Zealand
(a division of Pearson New Zealand Ltd)
Penguin Books (South Africa) (Pty) Ltd, 24 Sturdee Avenue, Rosebank, Johannesburg 2196, South Africa

Penguin Books Ltd, Registered Offices: 80 Strand, London WC2R ORL, England

www.penguin.com

First published 2006
1

Set in Monotype Baskerville by Palimpsest Book Production Limited, Polmont, Stirlingshire
Made and printed in England by Clays Ltd, St Ives plc

British Library Cataloguing in Publication Data
A CIP catalogue record for this book is available from the British Library

978-0-141-31855-4
0-141-31855-4

*This book is dedicated to Sophie, Catherine and Chloe,
always kind to their dad*

Contents

The devastating impact of the plague on fourteenth-century England is historical fact. The events and characters in this story are entirely fictitious.

I

Brother Rohan

Brind couldn't see the enemy, but he knew it was there. Any thicket, any rock, any overgrown hollow in the ground might conceal it. Lurking, waiting to pounce, to kill without teeth or sword. The sun was shining, hazy and lurid, and for almost the first day in a wretched twelve-month of rain and mud and blackened crops, it warmed the dog boy's back. But he couldn't relax. He hadn't felt like this for a long time. Hunted.

Brind's horse shied at a low branch and he swiftly steadied it, ready to defend himself, but nothing dropped from the branch except cankered leaves and last year's acorns, stunted and deformed by the sickly weather. Brind urged the horse on. The pack was far ahead of him now. Too far. Brind wanted to get close to the dogs, for his sake and for theirs. He was their huntsman, responsible to his master for their well-being, but they were also his companions, his friends. His family. He and they should be ready to fight this enemy together.

Then Brind heard Glaive, the pack leader. The hound's voice drifted up to him from the dense forest below. There was no sharp excitement in the call, as when scenting a deer or boar close by. Instead, it was a mournful sound, like the deep tolling of a funeral bell. And as Brind turned his horse and plunged down through the trees, the rest of the pack began to call with Glaive, sixty mastiffs giving anguished voice. Louder, louder, a nightmare choir filling Brind's head as he tried to reach them. The horse lurched and slithered beneath him and finally fell. Brind rolled clear as the horse scrambled upright again, but the dog boy ran on without the horse, his toes more at home in the soft earth than in stirrups.

The undergrowth before him became a tight mesh of saplings and brambles but Brind tore through it without heed, breaking out on to the stream bank where the hounds were massed, disturbed and confused, their great heads thrown back as they howled.

They were all alive, no outward sign of harm, and they licked at Brind and he ruffled their heads in mutual relief as he strode breathlessly into the pack. Glaive was sniffing at something on the ground and for a moment Brind thought perhaps the dogs had made a kill, after all. But Glaive's tail and ears were low and, as the last pack hound moved aside and Glaive raised his grizzled head,

2

Brind saw what the dogs had found. Not a deer, not a wild boar, but the master's wife, Lady Beatrice, face down in the mud, her limbs and body twitching as if jerked by strings.

The invisible enemy had struck. Plague had come to Dowe Manor.

The spider was large and deliberate, crawling slowly from the dusty hearth, across the pile of logs and up the wall towards the dark rafters high above. Sir Edmund Dowe hated spiders. Hated their silence, their sureness, their sudden speed and unpredictable scuttling. He hated the look of them too. This one had white markings on its bulbous body. The markings resembled a skull. Sir Edmund wanted to turn away but forced himself to continue staring, concentrating so that all his thoughts were on the spider. For if they were not, if they strayed, there was only despair. His wife was dying in the next room.

In the manor kitchen, Milda, the servant girl, was concentrating too. The egg she was holding was so newly laid it was still warm. That was good. Very good. And the marigold flowers heaped in the wooden bowl were also fresh. Carefully, Milda pierced both ends of the egg with a steel pin, then blew the contents on to the marigolds. The harmony of colours, egg yolk and marigold, was promising, she thought. And the yellow tansy too. Five flower heads of that. Then the honeycomb. And finally the jug of ale.

The glutinous mix glugged and sucked at the spoon as Milda stirred it. A little more ale, perhaps. The cooking fire was ready and waiting. She had worked hard to make it perfect. No flaring flames, just glowing, settled heat. The metal pot hissed as she tipped the contents of the bowl into it. The smell of hot, waxy honeycomb and marigold was strong but not unpleasant. Milda stirred and tried to remember how long the mix should cook for. Was it five hours or six? Five, surely, because there were five ingredients. But at all costs it mustn't burn. She turned the sand glass and continued stirring. At sunset she would take her mistress her first bowl of medicine, and at sunset tomorrow and the day after that. Then, on the third morning, Lady Beatrice would awake fit and well. Milda's mother had always claimed this recipe would cure anything.

A dark shadow passed over the cooking pot and Milda dropped the spoon, startled and fearful. Was she too late? Was Death already here? She turned. And screamed. Death was indeed standing on the threshold.

'God be with you, child.'

It was an unexpected greeting but Milda knew that Death was cunning. He smiled at the cooking pot.

'If that is dinner, you will take a small step towards a place among the angels by offering me a dish.'

He was plumper than Milda had always imagined. Not hollow-eyed and skeletal. Fat, in fact. But that was part of the cunning. Death, like the Devil himself, could assume many disguises.

Sir Edmund crashed into the bedchamber, mistakenly believing it was his wife who had screamed. But Lady Beatrice was long past screaming, even though the sudden light let into the room pierced her eyes like barbed arrows.

'Shut the door please, my lord.'

The small, thin girl sitting by the bed spoke respectfully and Sir Edmund quickly obeyed. The girl stood up, still holding Lady Beatrice's hand.

'Shall I leave you?'

Sir Edmund's courage almost failed him but he nodded, taking the limp white hand and squeezing it tight in a vain effort to stop his tears. He wasn't given to crying: weeping was for womenfolk. But there was no spider to fix his gaze on here. Only his beloved wife's once beautiful face, now disfigured by a large purple blotch across her cheek. Sir Edmund was ashamed to be glad that he couldn't see the rest, especially the loathsome black lump beneath her armpit.

Lady Beatrice opened her eyes again but didn't

recognize her husband. Her gaze was blank. Her mouth jerked slightly, though she was not attempting to speak. Mercifully, the horrible twitching that had overtaken her when out riding had more or less ceased. But it was a small mercy. It offered only a brief return of dignity, not health.

Sir Edmund cursed himself for the hundredth time. His wife had been unwell for several days before she'd insisted on that fateful ride. Sleepless, feverish, unable to keep food down. If only he'd confined her to bed then, forced her to rest; if only he'd fetched a doctor. The Earl of Arundel kept a doctor. But Arundel was twenty miles away and in any case the man's only cure was blood-letting. The sicker you were, the more blood he let out of you. Sir Edmund had no faith in blood-letting. Or was he just squeamish? No, no, his wife wasn't squeamish and she had no faith in it either. Her cure for everything was fresh air and fortitude. Only there was no fresh air this summer. Just the stink of rotting crops and dead animals. And now dead Englishmen. And women. His woman.

Was the foul air to blame? Sir Edmund needed to blame *something*, and in his heart he knew that it was pointless to blame himself. Bed rest and hot milk would not have saved his wife. Foul air, then. The cloud of foul vapours he had heard talked of, seeping invisibly across the countryside, killing those it touched. It came from the sea, caused by vast numbers of dead fish. Was that really possible? If so, why was his wife struck down and not him? Why had this deadly invisible cloud not touched everyone else at Dowe Manor? Milda, Aurélie, Brind. Even in the nearby hamlets, even in Dorset and Bristol, where it was said the devastation had first begun, not everyone had been touched. Some were chosen and some were not. But why had Beatrice been chosen? She was blameless. Faultless. Disease and death were commonplace, but this. *This*.

'It is the plague?'

Sir Edmund slowly raised his wet face from the bed and unclenched his fists. The voice behind him was unfamiliar, but calm, assured. It offered comfort. Sir Edmund turned his head. A large man, dressed in black and white, stood by the door. Black and white, but it was the black that dominated. The dark cowl and mantle, covering the man's head and shoulders and shading his face, gave him a sinister look, despite the understanding in his voice. Sir Edmund recognized the attire. A Dominican, a Black Friar. One of the holy preachers who tramped the rough roads of Europe and England, living on charity and spreading the word of God. Or their version of it.

The old knight remained on his knees, partly out of habitual reverence, partly because his joints had locked. He managed to speak.

'Yes, it is, Father.'

The friar bowed his head with a faint, modest smile.

'Brother,' he said, 'not Father. Brother Rohan.'

Despite his preoccupation, Sir Edmund was surprised that the holy man was apparently English. But then, just because the Pope and most of the saints were French, there was no reason why friars should be French as well.

'She is my wife,' said Sir Edmund.

He paused, forcing himself to acknowledge that the time had come. He must actually say the words.

'And she is beyond help in this world. Will you bless her and shrive her sins?'

Brother Rohan pushed back his cowl, revealing a face that was pink and sleek beneath its tonsure, and approached, but not too close, viewing Lady Beatrice from what he deemed a safe distance.

'Of course.' He laid a pudgy hand on Sir Edmund's shoulder. 'Though I'm sure her sins have been few.'

Sir Edmund steeled himself to be told that he should rejoice because his wife was on her way to Paradise. He didn't want Beatrice in heavenly Paradise. He wanted her here on dirty, imperfect Earth.

But the friar merely crossed himself and knelt

down. He smelt of rose water. As he began to mutter in Latin, the door behind him opened a crack.

'Aurélie!'

The small thin girl jumped and moved away from the door as Milda hissed her name along the passageway. Milda beckoned sharply and Aurélie felt obliged to obey.

In the kitchen, Milda had returned to vigorously stirring her concoction of marigolds and honey, as if there were still time for it to make a difference.

'My lady is dying,' said Aurélie flatly, implying the futility of Milda's efforts.

'Miracles happen,' said Milda. 'A man of God's just arrived. That's a miracle for a start.'

Aurélie didn't think so. And she wanted fervently to return to the bedchamber. She felt she should be there when Lady Beatrice actually died. Not because she wanted her to die, quite the opposite. But Aurélie had been absent at her real mother's death, outside Calais three years ago. The guilt had stayed with her. She needed to say a proper farewell to the English lady who had given her a home.

Brother Rohan quietly raised his head. He had chanted all the Latin he needed to chant, more or less, and a knight of Sir Edmund's middling, uneducated kind was unlikely to notice whether he had or not.

The friar considered the dying lady and hoped she would stop breathing soon. Being shut in a room with the plague made him uneasy, whatever the potential benefits. The chamber itself was simply furnished, almost frugal, but there was promise in the lady's jewellery, which looked old, probably handed down from richer generations, and in the furs and silks thrown aside from the bed.

Next to the friar, Sir Edmund still had his head bowed, whether in silent prayer or dumb grief Brother Rohan was unable to tell, though he suspected the latter, which also was promising. He could work on grief. Subtle conversation with the lumpish kitchen maid had told him all he needed to know: there were no children. The girl who had looked at him so disagreeably when he'd brushed her aside in the passage just now was unrelated. And French.

Brother Rohan was distracted by the barking of dogs. A whole pack of the brutes by the sound of it. He vaguely remembered noticing what he now realized must be kennels as he'd arrived at Dowe Manor. He'd assumed at the time that they were a row of pigsties, and had been looking forward to pork for dinner.

Suddenly Sir Edmund cried out beside him and

fell forward against the bed, clasping Lady Beatrice's hands. Her body had gone rigid, her back slightly arched, her mouth and eyes fixed in a horrible gape. Brother Rohan had missed the moment: the lady was dead.

Brind let the last batch of hounds into the feeding pen and watched that each of them got its fair share at the trough, especially Gabion, son of Glaive. For Gabion was a continual worry.

His birth, after Glaive's mating last year with Ballista, finest of the female mastiffs, had been eagerly awaited. But Gabion had defied expectation in all the wrong ways: he was small, he was weak and, most startling of all, he was jet black. In the muscular world of brown mastiffs, he stood out as an oddity, or would have done had he been big enough to be visible. This had been Brind's greatest and constant concern before Gabion was weaned: to keep him in sight in the whelping box, to save him from being inadvertently crushed by his bulkier brothers and sisters and even his mother. Gabion had survived, but that was the best that could be said about him. Almost nine months after weaning, he remained a conspicuous runt.

A more ruthless huntsman than Brind would have disposed of the puny mis-coloured pup at birth. Sir Edmund, who prided himself on the uniform perfection of his hounds, certainly would have done had Brind suggested it. But from the start, Brind had treated Gabion as if he were special rather than a special disappointment and, despite the sniggers and finger-pointing of occasional visitors, Sir Edmund hadn't interfered. He had to admit that, at the very least, Gabion was alert and affectionate. The dog boy knew best.

'Who is that?'

Brother Rohan was gazing across the yard at the strange youth crouched on his haunches in the dirt. His hands, with their long black nails, made Brother Rohan think of paws. And his teeth, when he showed them, were as pointed and sharp as those of the dog he was playing with. A small black dog. Brother Rohan was deeply suspicious of black dogs.

Standing beside the friar, Sir Edmund was taking deep breaths. He wanted to be with Beatrice but Brother Rohan, having murmured a prayer for the dead, had drawn him from the bedchamber. Milda and Aurélie were in there now, doing whatever women did in such circumstances. At the start and finish of life, at birthings and deaths, men were always excluded. But at least Sir Edmund knew that, when he was readmitted, his wife would appear more as he would wish to remember her, rather than the grotesquely twisted wreck of her dying seconds.

'The boy.' Brother Rohan's voice was slightly sharper. 'Who is he?'

'Brind,' replied Sir Edmund, without interest. 'My huntsman.'

'Your huntsman?' The friar looked at Sir Edmund in cool disbelief. 'Has he been in your service long?'

'Since he was a pup,' said Sir Edmund, then corrected himself. 'A baby. He was found in the stables, abandoned in a litter of mongrel whelps.'

Suddenly, he wanted to talk about Brind, after all. Perhaps if he talked enough about everyday things, normality would reassert itself, and Beatrice would walk out into the yard and ask if he was ever going to drag himself away from his precious hounds and come indoors to supper.

'Always been good with the dogs,' continued Sir Edmund. 'Understands them. Fourteen years now.'

'Indeed? He looks no more than ten.' Brother Rohan paused. 'The gift of perpetual youth, perhaps?'

There was no humour in the unblinking little eyes, but Sir Edmund assumed the friar was joking and shrugged.

'Just did all his growing early, that's all. Like a dog.'

Brother Rohan could feel the excitement growing inside him: the peculiar mix of dread and elation that came with discovery.

'And his companion? The black cur with him? When did that arrive?'

Arrive? A strange way of putting it. Sir Edmund shrugged again.

'Born last year.' He tried to find something good to say about Gabion.

'Unusual little thing.'

Brother Rohan looked straight at him, and there was something in the look that deeply disturbed Sir Edmund.

'And now the plague is here,' said the friar.

He sounded almost pleased.

Brind stood in the bedchamber with his head respectfully bowed. It was the first time ever that he'd been in this room and he felt uncomfortable, an intruder. Lady Beatrice, dressed in white linen, lay on the smooth, lavender-fresh bed. She was pale and serene, the purple blotch on her face already fading in death.

'I put some flour on her cheek to make it look nicer,' whispered Aurélie.

She was standing beside Brind, having fetched him from the kennels. She had already said her own goodbye to the dead lady; and thank-you. In the end, she'd had to say both to an unresponding corpse, but she'd told herself that Lady Beatrice's spirit was still present and could hear her, even though the body was cold.

Brind said nothing. He had known that Lady Beatrice was going to die, from the moment he'd found her, twitching in the mud, a week ago. The invisible enemy had claimed her. He was sad, he would miss her because she had always been kind to him, but she had never been involved with the dogs which were Brind's life, so her death would make no practical difference. Or so he thought.

'You know this is the Devil's work?'

Brother Rohan spoke with quiet certainty. He believed in God, but he believed even more in the Devil. And the Devil was here at Dowe Manor. He felt it strongly.

'The Devil?'

The old knight, leaning on the paddock fence beside him, seemed bewildered, lost. It was Brother Rohan's duty to guide him into the light.

'Do you think it is God's will that your lady should die so horribly and before her time?'

It was a difficult question to answer.

'Do you think it is God's will that half of England has already died a similar death?'

Even more difficult. God's will was unfathomable. Sir Edmund had never tried. Surely it was blasphemous to do so? One could rail against foul air but not God.

'Do you not understand, my lord, that this Earth

is the Devil's chosen battleground?' The friar shifted closer. His breath was hot in Sir Edmund's ear now. 'That since he was cast out from Heaven it has been his constant purpose and pleasure to taint, to spoil, to destroy God's every creation, and that mankind, being God's greatest joy, is also the Devil's greatest prize? He delights in your suffering, my lord. He rejoices.'

Sir Edmund felt inexplicably trapped. It seemed utterly wrong to be discussing the Devil and Beatrice in the same breath. Or was it, in fact, the Devil's presence that was so agitating him? He glanced swiftly round, but there was no leering horned beast, no whiff of fire and brimstone, only the stifling scent of rose water. He crossed himself hastily and stumped away from the kennels and out into the forest, heading for the small glade with its great fallen oak where he and Beatrice had always gone, since before they were married, to be alone together. But there was no respite for Sir Edmund now. Not from the Devil, or from Brother Rohan. The holy man was soon at his shoulder, speaking in his ear again. Brother Rohan preferred this intimate approach. Sermons worked well with a crowd, but with individuals it was more effective to act like a conscience. A small voice of reason. Calm. Logical. Tireless. Impossible to resist in the end.

'Do not expect to *see* the Devil here, my lord.'

He had noted Sir Edmund's sudden fearful look a few moments ago. 'He is far more subtle than that. Why do you keep a French girl in your household?'

The question disconcerted Sir Edmund still further. As if the friar had been discussing the Crusades and then suddenly asked the price of corn.

'She saved my life,' he replied simply. 'During the wars. Twice.'

Brother Rohan nodded knowingly before speaking again.

'You understand there are many witches in France? Many agents of the Devil.' He paused. 'Especially young girls.'

The insinuation was clear. And the normality Sir Edmund had been desperate to cling on to was beginning to spiral out of reach. Aurélie? A witch?

'How did she save your life, my lord?' The friar's voice was quiet, controlled, despite the eagerness within.

'First in a fire. Then at sea. In a storm.'

'Ah.' Brother Rohan smiled grimly in vindication. 'She controlled the elements.'

That wasn't how Sir Edmund remembered it. Aurélie had defied the elements rather than controlled them. She and Brind together. But then he had a sudden memory of the dog boy howling and laughing when the storm was at its height.

Standing on the flooded, plunging deck of the ship, completely without fear. Howling and laughing. Why had he been laughing? Never before had Sir Edmund questioned the dog boy's animal strangeness, or indeed Aurélie's changeability: civilized and courteous one moment, a wild vixen the next. But was that because there was nothing to question or because he'd been blind, naïve? He began to panic.

'I must speak to Beatrice,' he blurted.

And he turned and blundered away through the trees, back towards the manor, escaping from Brother Rohan, even though there was no escape from the thoughts and fears the holy man had sown. Brother Rohan didn't feel the need to keep pace. He was confident now.

As Sir Edmund approached the yard, he found Aurélie there. In her arms were the furs and silks from Beatrice's bedchamber. She was laying them on a pile of sticks and kindling.

'What are you doing?' Sir Edmund's voice was hoarse and harsh.

Aurélie looked up, startled.

'You told me to burn everything, my lord.'

Yes. He had said that. And he still wanted it. Wanted everything gone. Clothes, bedding, wall hangings. All of Beatrice's things. He couldn't bear the prospect of seeing them every day for the rest of his life.

Sir Edmund stumbled on without another word, then paused at the manor door and turned swiftly, as if trying to catch Aurélie out. She was staring after him. Why was she doing that? Crouched by the unlit fire, she looked smaller, sharper, more animal-like than he'd ever noticed before.

Sir Edmund went indoors, crossed the great hall and entered the bedchamber, kneeling beside his wife for the last time. He tried to speak, to say a fond and gentle farewell, but no words would come. No memories of a life shared. All he could think of was the injustice of the suffering he had witnessed without being able to help in any way. The fact that only Beatrice, the person who least deserved it, had been touched by this obscenely painful and disfiguring death. The more he thought about it, the more malice he could see. She must indeed have been evilly chosen. Tainted, spoilt, destroyed, just as Brother Rohan described. It *had* to be the Devil's work. And the Devil worked through those one least suspected.

Sir Edmund could smell smoke. Was it from the fires of Hell?

Brother Rohan could smell smoke too. And he was alarmed when he saw the source of it. The French girl had built a fire and was piling what were evidently the dead lady's possessions on it, including the silks and furs he had noted in the bedchamber. That seemed a terrible waste. The moth-eaten dimity wall hangings deserved to burn, but silk and fur had value. He quickened his step but was too late. The furs crackled and the pale silk flared and disintegrated the instant the heat touched it. Then he saw the cloth of gold.

A large roll of the gorgeous fabric lay incongruously in the dirt beside the bonfire. Richly textured silk, not like the flimsy stuff already burnt but almost as thick as linen and, most exciting of all, interwoven with gold. Its threads shimmered and danced before him and he couldn't take his eyes off it. Brother Rohan appreciated fine things. And coveted them greedily.

'Give that to me, child.' He spoke quickly but, as he thought, kindly, as Aurélie pulled the precious cloth towards the fire.

The girl just looked at him. There was insolence, defiance in her eyes. The garb and crucifix of a holy man meant nothing to her. She was undoubtedly a witch.

'The cloth is not to be burnt,' said the friar firmly.

'Everything is to be burnt,' replied Aurélie. 'My lord says so.'

She understood piercingly why Sir Edmund wanted it done. Especially the cloth of gold. The cloth merchant's recent visit to Dowe Manor had been a high point of happiness. Aurélie could still

20

see the merchant unrolling his wares one by one in the great hall. Holding the cloth of gold so that it caught the light. Offering rich, dark furs, the pelts of exotic beasts unknown in England or France, to Lady Beatrice so that she could caress her cheek with them. The laughter. Milda's delighted cooing. Brind's eagerness to help, his fascination with the furs. Sir Edmund's harrumphing as far too much silver changed hands. And his private smile as his wife wound the cloth of gold around herself and danced.

'Give it to me!'

Aurélie was jolted back to the unhappy present by the friar's sudden, savage anger. He lunged at her, grabbing her arm to prevent her from dropping the roll of cloth on to the flames.

'Devil's brat!'

She was skinny but strong, and struggled as he knew she would. As he heaved her aside, the cloth of gold fell and she deliberately kicked it towards the fire. Brother Rohan stretched out his own foot, trying to hook it clear, but as he did so the little witch sank her teeth into the thick, rough wool of his habit and clung to it like a dog. Barked like a dog too. Without opening her jaws. A thrill of fear passed through Brother Rohan at this phenomenon. Then he realized that the barking came from a real dog. It was the small black cur that he'd seen in the yard earlier, with Sir

Edmund's unlikely huntsman. And now it was jumping at him. The friar felt himself being pulled down under the weight of the girl on one arm and the dog on the other. The huntsman was there as well, also barking. The whole Devil's brood.

Brother Rohan squealed in pain and panic as the dog's teeth nipped his fleshy arm. Truly, the hounds of Hell were upon him! He rolled perilously close to the fire in his efforts to break free, feeling the heat of the ashes on his face and the scratching of the dog's hard nails on his bare legs.

'Witch!' he squealed. 'She-devil!'

He expected the dog's fangs to seek out his neck but instead the beast was suddenly dragged from him, as was the girl. Sir Edmund had come to his rescue.

'Go to your chamber!'

The old knight virtually threw Aurélie towards the manor house, then yelled at Milda, who had followed him outside.

'Lock her in!'

Aurélie was genuinely frightened. She had never seen Sir Edmund so enraged. But more shocking than the anger, or the sword in his hand, was the look of utter loathing. Sir Edmund appeared suddenly to hate her, and Aurélie realized why.

'I'm no witch, my lord!' she cried passionately. 'This holy man's no better than a thief!'

But the loathing in Sir Edmund's eyes didn't change.

'Lock her in!' he repeated.

Milda took Aurélie's arm uncertainly, but Aurélie didn't struggle. She fled indoors, sobbing.

Sir Edmund was clutching Gabion's collar and glaring fiercely at Brind now. Brind knew he was at fault for not controlling Gabion, but the truth was he'd never been able to control him, not in the instinctive, natural way in which he was able to command the rest of the pack. Especially where Aurélie was concerned. Gabion's desire to protect Aurélie always overcame his obedience. Though why Aurélie had been fighting the holy man, Brind didn't understand.

'Gabion bad,' he growled apologetically, as he stepped forward to take the dog. But he received such a violent shove across the chest from the flat of Sir Edmund's sword that he staggered backwards again and almost fell on the remains of the fire.

Sir Edmund said nothing, ignoring Brind's confusion, but Brother Rohan was on his feet again and more than ready to speak. He had wrestled with the Devil and the warm ash on his lips gave savour to his triumph.

'The only safe thing, my lord,' he said in a clear, firm voice, 'is to kill them. Witch. Devil's boy. Dog. The whole brood. They have done their work here.

It cannot be undone. But it can be revenged. Destroy them, my lord. They are all the Devil's weapons. Strike them from his hand so they cannot be used again!'

He could hear his voice rising, but it was impossible to suppress the excitement. He gazed at Brind, expecting the dog boy's pointed teeth to become fangs and the dirty fingernails to extend into claws, but nothing happened. Nor did the black cur snarl fiendishly and breathe brimstone. Even in defeat, the Devil did not reveal himself, such was his cunning.

'See how they have spilled the blood of a man of God!' cried Brother Rohan, thrusting his arm towards Sir Edmund, the tiny red puncture marks vivid on his pallid skin. 'Kill them!'

Brind smelt sweat and rose water as the holy man brushed past him.

Sir Edmund was staring at the smouldering bonfire, and glanced only briefly at the friar's wound. Then he looked up at Brind again, and Brother Rohan exulted as the heavy sword rose.

'Go,' said Sir Edmund to the uncomprehending dog boy. 'Take Glaive and go.' He pointed the sword shakily into the distance. 'Far away from here. Never return. Never.'

Then he threw his sword on to the ashes, and Brother Rohan stepped hastily backwards to avoid the flying sparks.

2

The Charcoal Burner

Brind had no possessions. Nothing to take with him and nothing to leave behind, except his imprint on the bracken in the kennel sleeping lodge. Even the belt around his waist and the mastiff at his heel belonged to his master.

He had been told by that master to go far away and he was doing simply that. He judged that if he walked along the forest track until he dropped, he would have gone far enough. Brind knew he was being punished but, in his doglike way, he could only associate that punishment with his most recent action, which had been to lose control of Gabion and allow the holy man to be bitten. It seemed an extreme penalty, but Brind had no inkling that it was permanent. He had been ordered never to return but assumed that meant he must wait until summoned. He would be sent for. Probably tomorrow.

As for Brother Rohan's calls for death and revenge, holy men often spoke in strange ways.

Brother Rohan had been angry at being bitten. Brind made no connection with the other, deeper tragedy at Dowe.

Aurélie kicked the door until her toes bled. Then lay face down on her narrow bed until her tears had soaked the straw of her mattress. When there were no more tears left, she briefly wished she *was* a witch, with power to fly through doors and walls as if they were made of gossamer. But that wish frightened her and she hastily unwished it, in case it came true, for although witches had freedom of a kind, it was a false freedom: their souls belonged to the Devil.

The immediate future frightened Aurélie too, as she calmed down. From her tiny slit of a window, she had glimpsed Brind's banishment and heard Brother Rohan's calls for her death. If the holy man's oily words and unblinking eyes had turned Sir Edmund's mind, what would happen when the door did open?

'This land has not been consecrated, my lord,' said Brother Rohan. Then, as if translating for the simple knight, he added, 'It is not holy ground.'

'I want to bury her here.'

Sir Edmund's voice was strained but dogged. They were standing in the forest, by the fallen oak. His and Beatrice's fallen oak.

'However,' said Brother Rohan, 'I am em-powered by His Holiness the Pope to consecrate ground. In certain deserving cases.' This was a lie, but often a useful and profitable one. 'And if, my lord, you were to establish a small chapel on the site, and endow a chantry, well, your piety would be proven beyond doubt, and the soul of your dear departed unquestionably saved. Not to mention your own.'

He always found it prudent to mention the living as well as the dead where salvation was concerned.

'I have no money to endow a chantry.'

Sir Edmund didn't want to build a chapel and install some bloodless priest in it, singing holy mass forever and a day. Did God listen to such things? He didn't appear to have listened to Sir Edmund's heartfelt pleadings. Why then should He listen to the mechanical droning of a paid cleric?

'My wife was a good woman. I have no fear for her soul. As for my own . . .' Sir Edmund shrugged dismissively and began to dig. But then it struck him that he was using the self-same spade with which he had dug another grave, two years earlier. For Tullo, Brind's predecessor as huntsman. The cruel, unhappy man who had tried to murder him, only to be thwarted by Brind and Aurélie. The self-same Brind and Aurélie who were now condemned as agents of the Devil. Doubt and confusion rose again, swirling around Sir Edmund like the cold sea in a sinking ship. He knew that he had been seized by madness. But had he been mad to suddenly believe that Aurélie was a witch, and Brind and Gabion demons; or mad to have taken so long to realize their hellish purpose? Had grief or the Devil manipulated his senses? He could still hear Aurélie sobbing in her room. A distraught twelve-year-old child. He could still picture Brind, loping obediently away into the endless forest. The faithful dog boy. He dug deeper into the dark, cold earth.

Brother Rohan left him to it. The real business would be more easily finished without the indecisive old knight.

The manor was silent, subdued, when the friar returned to it. Even the chickens in the yard and the hounds in their kennel paddock made no sound as he approached.

The roll of cloth of gold still lay across the dead bonfire, where the she-devil had kicked it, a large, ugly black bite taken out of it by the flames. It was ruined, worthless, and its wilful destruction added venom to Brother Rohan's zeal.

The imbecile servant girl was in the kitchen as before.

'Is the witch still locked up?' demanded the friar.

Milda nodded fearfully. She was in awe of Brother Rohan, and terrified to be in the same house as a witch. She did not doubt that Aurélie was a witch. Brother Rohan said she was. And there had always been signs: in the first place, she was French.

'And are there men here?' asked Brother Rohan urgently.

'Men, Father?'

She insisted on calling him Father. He didn't mind. It showed proper respect.

'Men who will strike a blow against the Devil and his works. Call them, gather them. Now, child, now!'

He was becoming impatient with Milda's gawky slowness, despite her deference. He wanted the witch dead before Sir Edmund returned. Then there could be no more wavering.

'Fetch men!'

But Milda didn't need to, for, as the friar spoke, they both heard the sound of hooves. Brother Rohan hustled before her into the yard, where a fierce-eyed little man was reining in a sorrel mare. Brother Rohan immediately liked the look of him, sensing self-confidence and a hot temper. Milda recognized him as Lifford, the miller, a freeman who lived in the creaky, dank mill house two miles away, and beat his wife.

There were six other men with him, all on foot, labourers from the hamlet close to the mill. News, like the plague, travelled fast.

'We've come to pay our respects,' said Lifford,

eyeing the Black Friar and looking beyond him for the absent Sir Edmund. Then he dug the quarterstaff he was carrying into the ground and used it to vault from his horse.

It was a trick Milda had seen him perform before. Typical of him, she thought, to swagger even at such a moment. But Brother Rohan didn't seem to mind. He fell on his knees with eyes closed and hands raised to the sky.

'God be praised for sending me an army!' he cried.

The labourers fell to their knees too, expecting a prayer for the departed soul of their master's wife, and, if they were lucky, for their own stricken families. But Brother Rohan had no time for the troubles of the poor. Unless they could be used to his own ends. He stood up, strode forward and took the quarterstaff from Lifford, who had not knelt down. Brother Rohan swept the staff around the group of hapless peasants.

'Has any of you suffered as your master suffers?' he asked. 'Are your hearts heavy with despair?'

They nodded and mumbled, and Brother Rohan looked to Lifford for a translation. The miller took the staff and walked behind the kneeling men, tapping each in turn as if they were dumb beasts, his dumb beasts. 'A wife, a son, a brother, all dead or dying.' He looked at Brother Rohan, his voice sharp. 'Why?'

'Because plague does not fall with the rain,' replied the friar calmly. 'It steals in through your doorways by design. The Devil's design.'

His eyes held those of the lowly creatures still on their knees before him.

'Who else comes through your doorway?'

They looked at each other, perplexed. Then they looked at Milda. Brother Rohan looked at her too.

'No, I don't!' she cried in alarm, suddenly realizing the implication, then pointing with a desperate finger.

'Not to your cottage, I don't, or yours, or yours. Aurélie brings the eggs, not me!'

The name was out before she realized it. There was a brief silence.

'The French she-devil visits these unfortunate creatures and their families?' asked Brother Rohan softly.

He was smiling at Milda now, and she felt reassured. Guilty but safe. She blushed deeply and nodded, then nodded again and went on nodding, even though Brother Rohan had turned away.

'Then I have the cause of your affliction trapped!' cried the friar at the men, as if a blinding truth had been suddenly revealed to him. 'The Devil's own child, grown like a canker-worm in the heart of this place, who strikes down whoever the arch-fiend chooses, high or low! I have a witch. Come with me and *kill* the witch!'

'Kill the witch!' echoed Lifford, brandishing the quarterstaff. He had never liked the French girl. She was kind to his wife behind his back, undermining his power in his own domain. Lifford wanted more power, not less. And the looks the girl had given him recently could only have been inspired by witchcraft.

'Kill the witch! Kill the witch!' he exhorted, and Brother Rohan knew that he'd been right in his judgement of the miller.

But the labourers were infuriatingly slow to respond to the call. They were fond of Aurélie, French or not, and though they shambled to their feet, they showed no inclination to rush after Brother Rohan towards the house. Lifford strode round in front of them.

'You butter-livered clods!' he cried. 'Can you not hear the Devil laughing at you? Can you not hear the little *witch* laughing?'

They couldn't.

'Is this how you respect a man of God?' sneered the miller. 'Do you call this holy man a liar?'

This was a question with dangerous implications.

'Well?' asked Brother Rohan with calm severity. '*Do* you?'

They dared not.

'Kill the witch!' roared Lifford, banging the quarterstaff on the ground for want of a drum, and, raggedly at first, then in full voice, the rest of the men joined in, before surging after him towards the house.

'Kill the witch! Kill the witch!'

For a mad moment Milda was terrified that they were coming for her after all, but they rushed past.

'Kill the witch!' Milda heard herself crying. 'Kill the witch! Kill the witch!'

In the passage, Brother Rohan paused until his now eager, vengeance-seeking band had massed behind him. The key was in the chamber door and, as he slowly turned it, the murderous chant subsided, the men suddenly apprehensive.

Brother Rohan threw open the door. He expected to be confronted by the hissing, spitting she-devil, or, if she had decided on subterfuge, a tearful waif, hunched helpless and appealing in the far corner. But he saw neither, just a brief flash of something low and fast on the floor, like a wild animal whipping past the hem of his habit.

Those at the back had seen nothing, and only the sound of Aurélie scrambling to her feet behind them and racing off alerted them to her escape. Now they saw her for the first time. It was definitely the French girl. Again they hesitated, remembering the many sweetmeats she had brought their children, her cheerful help with the harvest; but Brother Rohan seemed to read their thoughts.

'Do not be deceived,' he hissed. 'If she escapes, you will have not a child left alive among you.'

'Kill the witch!' they cried with renewed resolve.

In the yard, Milda was moving her feet in a strange little dance, completely lost in her own chant.

'Kill the witch, kill the witch, kill the witch,' she sang.

Then the witch hurtled from the house and collided with her, and Milda shrieked.

Aurélie struggled free of Milda's skirts and tried to grab the reins of Lifford's horse, but the animal reared and shied violently away from her. The men were out of the house now, grabbing billhooks and pitchforks as weapons, spreading around the yard to cut off her escape. There were no gaps. Aurélie hesitated a second, then ran straight at a wooden fence, clambered swiftly and dropped into the leaping mass of dogs beyond.

Agitated by the commotion in the yard and the smell of strangers, the mastiffs were now in full, ferocious voice, teeth bared, jaws dripping. As Lifford made a tentative move to climb the fence, they hurled themselves at him, snapping at the quarterstaff as he swung it at Aurélie's head.

Lifford had the brief satisfaction of impact as the tip of the staff struck the she-devil across the cheek, but then he was all but pulled into the paddock after her as two hounds clamped their fangs around the staff. He leapt backwards from the fence, dragging the quarterstaff with him. The smooth shaft had been wetly gouged by the dogs' teeth, and he rammed it angrily through the bars of the fence in retaliation, only for more of the polished wood to be splintered.

The other men were edging around the paddock, trying to keep Aurélie in view. Brother Rohan fervently hoped the mastiffs would tear her to pieces. To be able to present her death to Sir Edmund as an accident, or, even better, self-inflicted, would save any further tiresomeness. The witch would be dead but the contrary knight would be unable to blame Brother Rohan.

A shout of glee went up from the witch hunters as Aurélie, unbalanced by the blow from the quarterstaff, staggered and fell, sucked under the tide of jostling hounds. But Aurélie knew what she was doing. The mastiffs would not harm her. Brind had trained them well. Hidden in the smelly forest of dogs' legs and bellies, she crawled towards the nearest sleeping lodge.

Inside, the fresh bracken on the benches was cool and fragrant, but it brought no comfort. Brind had spread the bracken for his beloved hounds only hours ago, just as Aurélie had seen him do every day since he had brought her, a homeless orphan, to Dowe Manor. Since he had brought her to safety and hope. And now he was gone.

Banished. Brind banished! Aurélie wiped the blood from her throbbing cheek and squeezed herself through the slimy open drain at the end of the lodge.

The drain emptied on to the midden behind the kennel cooking hut. From there it would be a short sprint into the trees. Aurélie couldn't draw breath because of the stench, but she paused a moment on the dung heap, listening, trying to establish her pursuers' whereabouts.

The entire pack of hounds was still in the exercise paddock and, amid their barking, Aurélie could hear occasional shouts from Lifford and the men. She must go now, before they realized there was no chewed and trampled corpse beneath the mastiffs' feet. Aurélie sprang forward but, as she did so, she was flattened on her face in the dung. She squirmed sideways under the weight of her attacker and, rolling over, found herself glaring up not at a triumphant witch hunter but at Gabion. The black dog barked in her face and wagged his tail, then bounded off into the trees, turned and barked again. Aurélie followed.

Sir Edmund walked the width of the great hall, paused and walked slowly back. He looked up at Brother Rohan.

'Vanished,' he said, in a tone that, if not quite disbelieving, still suggested a hurtful difficulty in accepting the word of a man of God.

'Into thin air,' said Brother Rohan. 'As I have explained. She leapt among the dogs, yet when the dogs removed themselves, she was gone.'

How many more times did he have to tell this slow, dithering fool? For a moment he regretted having come to Dowe. He had nothing to show for his efforts. An entire Devil's brood had escaped him. It wasn't his fault, but it was a blemish on his hitherto-perfect record.

Nor was there any sign of earthly reward. Sir Edmund was clearly disinclined to endow a chantry. The furs and silks were burnt. The jewels buried with the wife. The cloth of gold. Brother Rohan tried not to dwell on the cloth of gold, but it was hard, very hard. It would have paid for so many fine dinners. He had no qualms about looking after his stomach. Brother Rohan was a soldier of God and soldiers had to eat.

'It is commonplace for a witch to vanish,' said the friar. 'A last resort, but quite within their powers.'

Sir Edmund wondered why, if this were true, so many witches in France allowed themselves to be burnt alive. But he said nothing. He was weary of thinking. And he was weary of the Black Friar, who had seemed to provide reasons, and someone to blame – the things Sir Edmund had craved – but who, somehow, had reduced him to a deeper desolation than before. It hardly seemed possible.

The old knight sat in his chair beside the hearth. The chair on the other side, Beatrice's chair, gazed emptily back at him, but he didn't take his eyes off it. Eventually he spoke.

'I think you should go, Brother Rohan,' he said quietly. 'No doubt you have God's work to do elsewhere.'

Aurélie regretted having kicked her door so long and pointlessly. Her damaged toes chafed so much that she threw away her shoes and walked barefoot.

Gabion thought this was a game and for several minutes kept bounding back and forth along the track, retrieving the shoes, until Aurélie lost her temper and hit him on the nose with one of them. Gabion seemed to think this was a game as well and only by ignoring him completely did Aurélie eventually get some peace.

Gabion was a peculiar dog. Not simply because of his blackness, but because he had failed to grow up serious-minded like a mastiff should. This perpetual puppy-hood was partly Aurélie's fault. Brind had given Gabion constant care and attention, but Aurélie had to admit that it was she who had spoilt him. Titbits between meals, little afternoon sleeps on her bed, chasing butterflies in the woods when he should have been learning the discipline of a proper hunt.

Unintentionally, she had blunted Brind's authority as pack leader, though Brind was generally good-natured about it. Indulgent, even. But then, perhaps Gabion would have been untrainable even without Aurélie to distract him. He was an independent outsider. As Aurélie considered herself. It gave them a bond: Aurélie liked to think of Gabion as her dog. And he wasn't completely useless as the hunting animal he was supposed to be. He had the sharpest sense of smell in the entire pack. Aurélie was confident that he would be able to scent Brind and lead her to him.

The charcoal burner was a black and shiny man, like a lump of charcoal himself: as if he had fallen out of the smouldering stack behind him. He grinned and nodded at the dog boy across the cooking pot, his three remaining teeth glowing in the firelight. Then he dipped his hand into the pot and picked out a piece of stewed rabbit, which he handed to Brind, before cackling raucously as the dog boy found the meat too hot to hold.

Glaive sat up hopefully and licked his lips by way of a hint, but Brind juggled with the meat until it was cool enough to pop into his own mouth. Glaive subsided again. He knew he always had to wait, but there was never any harm in trying.

'Go far?' asked the charcoal burner, as he sucked rabbit from its bone.

Brind shook his head. 'Come far. Stop here.' Then he added, 'Gabion bad.'

The charcoal burner glanced warily at the hungry dog beside the boy.

Brind shook his head again. 'Glaive good.' He stroked the dog's muzzle and allowed him to lick the warm juice from his fingers.

The charcoal burner was a solitary man with little more language than Brind himself.

'Shared rabbit ago,' he said after a while, then counted on his fingers. 'Seven nights.'

'Holy man?' asked Brind cautiously.

The charcoal burner shook his head. 'Merchant.'

He dipped his fingers in the simmering pot again, and indicated for Brind to also help himself, then exploded into more cackling at the boy's attempts to do so. He did enjoy the occasional company of strangers.

Brind woke suddenly in the night. He could hear scuffling noises. Then a sharp cry made him sit up. Glaive was already awake beside him, tensed and growling.

The sounds were coming from the direction of

the cooking fire. The fire was dead but a small patch of the nearby charcoal stack glowed through its coat of packed earth, and in the dim red light Brind could see something moving on the ground.

At first he thought it was a badger but, as he crept closer, he realized it was human: the charcoal burner. The man was tossing and writhing in the half-sleep of a fever. Then he cried out again and his body began to jerk violently. Sudden, hideous twitchings that Brind had seen before, in another, distant part of the forest.

Glaive backed away, whining, but Brind forced himself forward until he was crouching close to the man. He reached out and, sensing his close-ness, the charcoal burner suddenly grabbed at the dog boy, as if clinging to another living being would somehow save his own life. His grimy fist was slippery with sweat as he held on to Brind's arm, and his breath, when he spoke, was sour with vomit. He managed only one word and Brind could have said it for him.

'Plague.'

The stars were clear and bright, and Aurélie tried to count them. She had told Gabion that the two of them should take turns at sleeping, but the dog had pretended not to notice when she tried to poke him awake. He was not the best of guard dogs, despite his sense of smell. So Aurélie remained on watch until the stars merged into a sparkling blanket, which slowly settled on her, and kept her warm as she dreamed that Brind and Glaive were just around the next corner. And the next. And the next.

By morning, the charcoal burner was cold and still. He had died much more quickly than Lady Beatrice.

Brind marvelled fearfully at how the enemy had managed to creep to the cooking fire without waking either himself or Glaive. Glaive heard everything, even when asleep.

The dark wounds that the plague inflicted were not as evident on the charcoal burner as on the white-skinned lady, but the swellings were the same. Everything was the same. And now Brind had a corpse to deal with. He had no means of burying the dead man, and it seemed wrong to prop him in his charcoal stack, even though it might have been what the man himself would have wished, so in the end Brind covered him with leaves and small branches, and retreated to the track from where he had first smelt the cooking fire the night before.

There he sat and waited uneasily, and Glaive lay beside him, dozing, snapping at flies, chewing roots, standing up occasionally and looking at

Brind with an expectant wag of the tail, unused to this strange inactivity.

Then at noon on the second day since dog and boy had been sent away from Dowe, Glaive set the wood pigeons clattering in the foliage overhead with a sudden bark. He was quickly on his feet, head raised, ears and nose straining to the west. Brind also stood up, gazing down the track, but could see nothing. He touched the hound's flank, releasing him to follow his senses, and Glaive raced away.

The forest was close on either side, the trees locking branches above the track, making a curved green tunnel of it, and Glaive had almost disappeared from sight when he came to a skittering halt, in collision with someone or something arriving just as fast from the opposite direction.

Brind gave a bark of joy as he recognized the gangly streak of black tangled in the mud with Glaive. By the time he'd run to them, the two dogs were upright again, circling each other, sniffing and soft-biting, tails thrashing in unison. Brind threw himself on them, laughing, arms round their necks, tumbling them over again and rolling with them into the damp, sweet leaf mould at the edge of the track.

Eventually the dog boy sat up, in the expectation of seeing one of the labourers from Dowe, or even

Sir Edmund himself on his horse, but there was nobody. He frowned at Gabion, as if the dog might explain, but then a figure came into view. A small, slight figure, not on horseback but on foot, and limping painfully.

Aurélie walked up to Brind and controlled a strong urge to collapse. She'd become increasingly angry with the dog boy for having made her walk so far.

'You're alive, then,' she said. 'That's good.'

Without another word, she trudged on until she reached a low mossy bank, flopped down on its relative comfort and closed her eyes. When she opened them again, Brind was standing over her with a leather bucket in one hand and a pile of last year's mildewed beech nuts in the other. It was too early for blackberries and the nuts were the best he could find on the forest floor. The leather bucket had belonged to the charcoal burner, and at least the water from the stream was clear and fresh. Aurélie drank and ate and, as usual, felt guilty. She always managed to be ungracious to the dog boy.

'Thank you,' she said, although chewing the nuts hurt her injured mouth.

Brind smiled. 'Go home now?'

Aurélie didn't look at him. 'Home?' she said.

The dog boy nodded. Then, misunderstanding her unhappy expression, he cradled his arms and grinned at her. 'Carry you.'

Aurélie shook her head. 'We can't go home, Brind. *You* can't go home.'

She hadn't prepared herself for how difficult this was going to be. She wished the dog boy would stop staring at her so blankly.

'You can't go home, Brind.'

He didn't speak again but, suddenly alarmed, dropped on his haunches close to her and tentatively pointed to the purple bruise on her cheek.

'Plague?' he growled.

'No, no, not plague. Just a bruise.'

She tried to find words he would understand.

'But the plague is why we can't go back. Sir Edmund sent you away because of the plague.'

Brind frowned. 'Gabion bad,' he said. 'Bite holy man.'

'Yes. Sir Edmund thinks Gabion is bad. He thinks I'm bad. He thinks you are bad. He thinks *we* killed Lady Beatrice.'

At least the dog boy seemed to register surprise at this. It was a start.

'He thinks we brought the plague, Brind. You, me, Gabion. Brother Rohan says the Devil sent us. He says we are plague bringers, and Sir Edmund believes him. That's why he sent you away. That's why you can never go home. Never.'

The dog boy said nothing. His dark eyes slid away from her, but otherwise he didn't move for

45

several seconds. Aurélie couldn't tell what he was thinking, but knew well enough that if he'd properly understood the words 'never go home', he would be heartbroken. She was not to realize the even darker thought churning in his mind, and when he suddenly stood up and walked away, she thought for a moment that he'd understood nothing after all and was about to march back along the track towards Dowe. Instead he headed into the trees, then began to run.

Aurélie swiftly followed. She could smell smoke, and when she reached the clearing to which Brind had run, she noticed the charcoal stack before anything else. Brind was standing by a heap of brushwood, and Aurélie jumped back in horror when he swept the branches aside. The dog boy gazed down at the leaf-strewn body of the charcoal burner, then looked up at Aurélie with a despair that shocked her even more than the unexpected corpse.

'Plague bringer,' he growled mournfully, pointing at himself. 'Kill charcoal burner.'

'No, Brind,' exclaimed Aurélie, and she instinctively put out her hand to touch him, but he backed sharply away.

'Plague bringer. Kill charcoal burner. Kill Lady Beatrice. Plague bringer. Plague bringer . . .'

He was nodding his head, as if trying to shake other words from his mouth, words that would

46

adequately express his devastation, but none would come. And when Aurélie stepped towards him, he stumbled backwards still further, his hands firmly out of her reach behind his back.

'Plague bringer!' he cried. 'Kill *you*!'

And with a last look of utter misery, he turned and fled.

3
The Village

Brother Rohan relished the change. Being a foot soldier of God was a painful duty; being a mounted warrior of God was inspiring. The horse that Sir Edmund had given him was not the fleetest-footed beast in the world: it lumbered along at its own pace. But it was imposing in size, and Brother Rohan saw nothing wrong in that. He also reasoned that the physical comfort of riding on horseback, rather than pounding the rough track in his sandalled feet, freed his mind for higher thoughts, encouraged contemplation.

He was contemplating now, though his mind had moved swiftly from the mysteries of God to the prospects afforded by the town of Horsham. He viewed towns as multiplications of manors: if he had identified a Devil's brood at Dowe, how many dozens were there to be rooted out in Horsham? And how much greater would be the acclaim and rewards to be modestly received? But he must arrive there before the plague. Fear was his most potent ally. After God, of course.

The friar dug his heels eagerly into the flanks of his newly acquired steed, even though he knew it wouldn't respond, and glanced sideways at his assistant, also newly acquired: Lifford, jogging busily along beside him on his sorrel mare. The miller carried the quarterstaff tucked under his arm, as if it were a lance and he a noble knight. He was nothing of the kind, but he had fire in his belly and a hatred of witches, and Brother Rohan had seen no reason to dissuade him from joining the war against the Devil, albeit in a subsidiary role. True, apparently he had abandoned a wife and several children in order to do so, but hardship and sacrifice were inevitable.

Lifford didn't speak to the friar as they rode. He had no illusions, other than that fate had been incredibly unjust in making him a miller rather than a man-at-arms or, at the very least, a huntsman. He wanted freedom, real freedom, recognition. And revenge, though the revenge was against life in general and was his only way of striking back against fate. Witches were useful in this respect. It was acceptable, indeed praiseworthy, to hate witches. He already hated Aurélie. The fact that she was now identified as a witch enabled him to be self-righteous as well as vicious. He wasn't convinced that she had vanished and harboured hopes of tracking her down. In the meantime, he had broken the shackles of Dowe and the daily grinding of corn. He was riding with the Black Friar into adventure. There would be more witches to be killed. And Horsham sounded a good place to start hunting for them.

Brind had touched Lady Beatrice's hand only once, helping her to mount her horse on the morning of her last ride. But it had been enough. He was to blame. The holy man said so, Sir Edmund said so, and now the evidence of Brind's own eyes had made it certain. He had touched the charcoal burner's hand over the cooking pot, as he'd been given his first scalding piece of rabbit. He was to blame. He curled himself tighter into a ball, his hands clasped to his chest so that he could touch no one else. Ever.

'Brind?'

Aurélie's voice was uncharacteristically soft and anxious. She'd never heard the dog boy cry. She'd assumed that he couldn't. But he was sobbing now, his voice a choked miserable yelp.

Gabion, who had tracked Brind down, now looked up at Aurélie, even his carefree spirit daunted, while Glaive, having acknowledged the new arrivals with a single bark, resumed nuzzling at the dog boy's unresponsive head. Aurélie knelt down.

'Brind, listen to me. You're not a plague bringer. You're not.'

She reached out to put her arm around him, but, as her fingers touched his sleeve, he exploded from the hollow in which he'd been lying and tried to flee again. Aurélie was quicker this time, though, and sprang after him, grabbing his hand and holding it tight, pulling him back. The dog boy howled and tried to shake himself free, but Aurélie took his other hand as well and stood firm in front of him as he trembled and panted and tossed his head in despair, like an animal in a trap.

'Don't run away, Brind. We have to stay together. We have to!'

Brind shook his head violently, forcing their locked hands into the air.

'Plague bringer . . . Plague bringer . . . Kill you . . .' he moaned sorrowfully.

'No, you won't give me the plague. You won't kill me. You won't, you won't . . .'

Aurélie surprised herself with her tenderness. And with her strength. She clung on, and gradually she felt Brind's resistance subsiding, and a little of his panic. But he continued to stare at their locked hands, as if expecting the dreadful purple stains to appear on her at any moment.

'And anyway,' said Aurélie, 'there are other things to think about.'

It sounded odd, a mundane thing to say, while

Brind was obsessed with being a cause of agonizing deaths, but it was true. And it might be a means of distracting him.

'We have to think about Sir Edmund. We have to *do* something. It's our duty.'

Duty was a word she knew he understood. She lowered her hands but didn't loosen her grip.

'The friar will have gone by now. Sir Edmund's alone at the manor, just him and Milda. That's not good, it's not safe. He's old, he's not thinking properly. He's vulnerable.' She tried to find another word for vulnerable. 'Someone could attack him. Attack the manor. You remember what the cloth merchant said?'

The merchant hadn't brought just furs and cloth of gold to Dowe; he'd brought stories too. Stories of soldiers coming back from the war. Reckless men, some of them no better than outlaws. Gangs roaming the English countryside.

'What if a gang of cut-throats came to Dowe?' asked Aurélie, as Brind looked up. 'What chance would Sir Edmund and Milda have?'

She didn't mention the plague, which had already wiped out most of the able-bodied men who might have helped defend the manor.

Brind was shaking his head violently.

'Can't go back,' he growled. 'Can't go back.' But the message was clearly getting through.

'No, we can't go back,' agreed Aurélie. 'But it's

better if we don't. It's better if we go to Garwood.'

The name seemed to mean nothing to Brind. Aurélie realized that he might never have heard it.

'Garwood Manor. Where Lady Alice lives. Lady Beatrice's sister. She can send some of her men to Dowe to protect Sir Edmund.'

Brind had stopped shaking his head. Aurélie pressed on.

'Garwood's not that far. Somewhere beyond Horsham, I think,' she added vaguely. 'Anyway, we can ask when we get to the town. Brind, it's our duty!' She squeezed his hands and stared earnestly into the doubtful dark eyes. 'I'm not just sitting here and waiting to die of the plague!'

Brind flinched slightly at the word, but Aurélie sensed that he wasn't going to run off again. Eventually, he turned his head, as if speaking to the dogs rather than to her.

'Find town,' he growled.

'Good day, my lord.'

The horseman smiled down at Sir Edmund. His companion said nothing.

'Good day.'

Sir Edmund hadn't been expecting visitors and didn't want any. His tunic was grubbier and more food-stained than usual, and his beard badly needed trimming. He continued less gruffly, however.

'Are you looking for work?'

They hardly seemed like wandering labourers, but it was worth asking.

The first horseman smiled again.

'Not the kind of work you'd be offering, my lord.'

'I haven't said what I'm offering.' Sir Edmund didn't like insolence. 'I need a huntsman. Someone who knows about dogs.'

The first horseman turned to his companion.

'Do we know about dogs, Kendrick?'

Kendrick shrugged. 'Woof, woof,' he said, and continued his apparently casual perusal of the manor house and its outbuildings.

'Sorry, my lord,' said the first horseman, with a shake of the head.

'Digging ditches?' asked Sir Edmund with tetchy sarcasm. 'Sowing, reaping? Bird scaring? The plague's been here, in case you hadn't noticed. My people are either dead or run away.'

Kendrick smiled down at Sir Edmund and tutted sympathetically. 'No sense of feudal duty nowadays.'

The old knight glared back. 'If you don't want work, what do you want?'

'Hospitality would be nice,' said Kendrick, looking away again. 'A jug of wine, a roast chicken or two.'

'I can offer you beer and beans,' said Sir Edmund. 'That's all we have.'

He should have felt humiliated by the confession, and it wasn't strictly true, but he didn't care. Suddenly, he didn't want this pair to get off their horses: he'd just noticed the swords tucked neatly beneath their saddle blankets. The dagger hilts inside their jerkins.

'Beer and beans, Kendrick?' asked the first horseman.

Kendrick made a small rude noise.

'Thank you for the offer, my lord,' said the first horseman politely, 'but we'll just continue on our weary way.'

Milda appeared in the house doorway as the two horsemen ambled off. Sir Edmund, watching till they were out of sight, heard them laugh, and was relieved that they'd gone.

Back in the kitchen, Milda's concoction of marigolds and honey still sat untouched, congealed in its bowl. Milda was certain that it would have saved Lady Beatrice if given in time and was reluctant to dispose of it in case the plague returned. Indeed, she had convinced herself that its presence in the kitchen would keep the plague away, like an orangey-brown talisman.

She tried not to think about Aurélie, whose memory somehow seemed less witchlike now that Brother Rohan had gone. But she missed Brind more.

Milda heard Sir Edmund approaching. In the

last few days he'd taken to sitting by the cooking fire rather than in the great hall, but although master and servant girl were now the only occupants of Dowe Manor, neither was comfortable in the other's presence. Milda scuttled out in search of eggs for the poor miller's wife and children.

Sir Edmund glanced at the bowl of marigolds and honey. Still there. Milda had never told him what it was for and he assumed it to be one of her less successful culinary efforts, eventually to be fed to the chickens. He wasn't at all hungry but knew he had to eat, so, as he sat down, he ladled himself a bowl of potage. It was the only thing he'd swallowed since Brind and Aurélie had gone: a broth so thin he didn't have to think about chewing.

The madness had passed. Sir Edmund had given Brother Rohan his second-best horse, not in gratitude but in order to be rid of him. The friar expected something and, despite the urgency of his mission as a soldier of God, had definitely been loath to move on without it.

Sir Edmund fervently hoped that the holy man and his self-appointed henchman, Lifford, would come across neither Aurélie nor Brind. It was the only thing he did feel fervent about. The rest was dull despair. He knew he should shake it off, but what was the point? What was the point of anything? Even his mastiffs, the finest pack in all of England, were too much effort. He fed and watered them daily, but that was it.

As for the manor itself, it had been hard enough to keep the land properly worked even before the plague, and Brother Rohan, had arrived. The sudden desertion of so many who owed him service did rankle, even if they were fleeing the plague. But feudal duty worked both ways. A lord was supposed to protect his people, and he had failed. Sir Edmund could do nothing about the plague; but he had banished Brind forever. And left Aurélie at the mercy of a witch hunt. Even the thin broth stuck in the old knight's throat.

The village appeared quite suddenly. Aurélie and Brind had been avoiding the track, just in case they should meet Brother Rohan, but Aurélie had tired of the endless ducking and weaving through trees and bushes. She was also hungry. They were all hungry, girl, boy and dogs, and could find nothing in the forest that even Brind could pretend was food. So they had taken the risk of rejoining the track. There was no guarantee that it would lead to the town, but if they met somebody they could ask. And now, here in front of them, was a village no doubt full of people who would know the way to Horsham, and perhaps have food to share, or even sell. Aurélie had taken the small gold ring from her finger several times, then pushed it back again. She didn't want to part with it, but it should be worth enough food to keep them going for days.

Curiously, no dogs came charging towards them as they reached the first houses. No barking and snarling, not even a distant yap. No urchins either, playing in the dirt. Perhaps they were helping in the fields. Perhaps everyone was helping in the fields.

Aurélie marched to the first closed, rickety door and knocked at it. There were always old women in villages, even when everyone else was working. They sat by the fire and span wool, or made oatcakes. Aurélie slid the ring from her finger and gently pushed the door open. The cottage was dark and empty; the fire on the hearth dead. No oatcakes, not even an old woman.

Brind was standing rigidly in the middle of the track, wanting nothing to do with the village or its inhabitants. He had gone along with Aurélie's plan but was far from convinced that he was not a lethal risk to anyone he met.

The dogs followed their noses from house to house but seemed to find nothing to excite their senses. Aurélie moved methodically after them, knocking, calling, peeping inside, then turning each time with a shrug at Brind. The village was deserted.

Beyond the last house, a larger building stood apart. A squat rectangle, poorly built of hardened clay, with a bell outside and a wooden cross nailed to its timber roof. Aurélie looked at Brind, who shook his head violently.

'It's a church,' hissed Aurélie, feeling impelled by the surrounding silence to speak quietly. 'You can't harm a church.'

The dogs held back, but Aurélie indicated sharply for Brind to follow her. Obviously the entire village was at worship.

The church door was shut and, although the latch rose easily enough, the door itself barely moved as Aurélie tried to push it ajar. Something was in the way. She could hear no priest saying prayers, no congregation coughing or shuffling, no fretful infants or bored, whispering children. Curiosity got the better of her. She gestured at Brind, and between them they slowly eased the door open, heaving aside whatever had been propped against it. The body of a woman, as old and bent as Aurélie could have wished to meet in the first cottage, fell sideways on the earthen floor at their feet, her vacant eyes lit briefly by the suddenly intruding sunlight.

Aurélie screamed, and went on screaming. Brind would have screamed too, but his voice was frozen, like his blood. The church was filled with death. Whole families huddled in every corner, on every patch of floor: dogs, goats, even a cow pressed among them, as if the entire village had sought shelter in the church. Refuge from some violent storm. But there had been no refuge; the dark stains and swellings of the plague were on every single person, except a tiny baby, still hanging from its mother's breast.

Aurélie forced herself to pick her way through the stiff, unfeeling bodies to where the baby's mother sat hunched against the east wall, beneath the only window, her lifeless hand clasping a small cross. Aurélie touched the baby. It was cold as ice. A small nightmare statue, like all the others that crowded silently around it.

Aurélie looked towards the door, expecting Brind to have run out, but he was standing where she'd left him.

'Have you been here before, Brind?' whispered Aurélie.

Her voice, though hushed, was savage. Not against the misguided dog boy, but against whoever, whatever, could cause such poisoned catastrophe. Brind didn't immediately understand the reason for the question, but he shook his head.

'Then you are *not* the plague bringer,' said Aurélie.

Only now did she become aware of the unspeakable stench in the church. But she refused to run from it. She walked slowly back to Brind, took his hand and led him outside, into life.

They walked in silence for several miles, careless of discovery on the winding track. From time to time, Aurélie squeezed Brind's hand, and eventually the shock began to thaw from their hearts and minds.

Brind understood that he could not have brought plague to the village. He didn't have to hide himself away forever, after all. The poor people in the church had been beyond help, but his master wasn't. Brind had a purpose, a duty. He and Aurélie would find their way to Garwood.

Aurélie sensed the renewed vigour in the dog boy's step and knew that some good, at least, had come out of the dreadful desolation they had witnessed.

Brind smelt the town before he saw it. Pigs, sheep, cattle, dead and alive. Rotting cabbages and fresh bread. Wood smoke, hot steel, leather. A pungent stew of man and beast and manufacture, heavily spiced with sewage.

Glaive and Gabion scented it too, and Gabion became nervous, glancing at Brind and Aurélie, his senses overpowered. Brind took off his belt and tied it to Gabion's collar as a makeshift leash, so that he could pull the reluctant dog forward.

The town was in a low valley, on a river, and, as it came into view below them, Aurélie thought it looked as primitive as it smelt. Little more than a bulging huddle of wooden huts, really. No surrounding wall, no castle; in fact, no stonework at all to speak of, other than a single church. But then, this was England, and nothing better could be expected.

'Come on,' she said to the hesitant Brind. 'I'm starving.' And she strode off down the hill towards the only bridge.

Brind had never been in a town before. The narrow streets and tottering buildings that almost shut out the sky above gave him the feeling of being indoors, underground even, as if he were entering some giant, complex burrow. Except that in animal burrows there were always quiet corners for the solitary. Here, every tunnel was full of noisy, jostling inhabitants, all constantly on the move, mostly in opposite directions.

Aurélie seemed perfectly at home, though, slipping easily through the crowds. When a bullock cart full of shrieking pigs ground and squelched to a halt ahead of them, blocking the entire width of the tunnel, she simply ducked and crawled underneath it. Brind and the dogs followed. The dog boy worried that they were going deeper and deeper into the burrow, with no apparent means of escape, but nobody took any notice of the new arrivals. In fact, Brind and Aurélie might have been invisible from the way everyone tried to hurry straight through them.

Unusually, Aurélie was following her nose. Her sense of smell wasn't as highly developed as that of the dogs or Brind, but she could sniff out good fresh bread from half a mile away, even if it wasn't French bread.

Around corners and down narrower and narrower tunnels she hurried, but when she came to the baker's shop, she didn't halt, or even slow down, only knocked a quartern loaf from the low trestle by the doorway, kicked it a few paces further, then swiftly scooped it up. Aurélie knew she was stealing, which was wrong, but they had no means of paying: her ring, her only valuable, was lost, probably lying dropped somewhere among the corpses in the village church. Besides, the English had stolen a million loaves from the French during the wars. What was one in return? Still walking, she picked off the dirt with her equally dirty fingernails, then tore off a hunk of bread and handed it to Brind. They perched on a pile of discarded sacks to eat their meal, tossing crusts to Glaive and Gabion, though there was plenty else for the dogs to forage for in the heaped refuse around them.

Aurélie was just starting to wonder where she might find some cheese, or perhaps a pastry, when she noticed that Brind had stopped eating. The dog boy was sitting quite still, his head raised.

'What's the matter now, Brind?' asked Aurélie. The tenderness hadn't lasted long.

Brind didn't reply. He could smell rose water.

4

The Devil's Mark

It was a fine thing to have an audience. Brother
Rohan surveyed the expectant, open faces below
him. Two hundred souls or more, the biggest
crowd since he had started his progress from the
west, had squeezed on to the rutted patch of
beaten earth that passed for a market square.
Trusting, pliant souls, just waiting to be told what
to believe. It wasn't only the power that Brother
Rohan enjoyed, the power to sway and direct. It
was the exhilarating knowledge that he was right.
He stretched out his arms and stood like a mighty
black-winged bird, waiting for silence.

'Brothers and sisters in God,' he cried, and was
deeply satisfied with the resonance in his voice.
'Why have I, a humble friar, come among you
today?' He paused, but for effect rather than an
answer. 'I have come to save you from the Devil.
As I have saved many others in this cursed land
of ours. For he is *close.*'

The humble friar paused again, dramatically.

65

'Listen. Do you hear his footfall? Do you hear his breathing?'

The hushed crowd listened fearfully, but Brother Rohan was shaking his head.

'No. You cannot hear the Devil. You cannot *see* the Devil. Only his works make him known. And what is the foulest of all his works but the plague!'

The anxious citizens of Horsham found relief in agreeing noisily, and, as they did so, Brind and Aurélie crept to the edge of the crowd. The dog boy sensed that they were at the heart of the burrow now, but they could see nothing: a wall of backs blocked their view of Brother Rohan, and the overhanging roof of an inn still kept out the light. The friar's voice floated to them, though, and Aurélie felt Brind's whole body tense: he was ready to flee. She clutched his hand, wanting to stay and listen. If they couldn't see Brother Rohan, he couldn't see them. Or Gabion and Glaive, gnawing at the chicken carcasses they'd unearthed in the refuse heap.

'Know who is the Devil's friend,' continued the holy man. 'Seek out those among you who would open the gates of Hell and let loose terror and death in this fine town. For unless you do, no citizen, however righteous, no maiden, no babe in arms, however innocent, is safe!'

And, as two hundred people murmured their unease and glanced suspiciously at their neighbours, Brind was knocked to the ground by a blow between his shoulder blades.

So sharp was the pain, Brind thought he must have been shot with a crossbow bolt but, as he scrambled to his knees, he heard Lifford's voice. The miller laughed, and hooked him over, then jabbed the quarterstaff down hard into Brind's midriff, pinning the dog boy to the ground.

'Hold them!' he cried, as those nearest to the sudden commotion turned.

'These are your friends of the Devil! These are your plague bringers! Hold her!'

He was yelling urgently now, as Aurélie flew at him, her nails scratching at his face. But those who dared weren't quick enough and, as women shrieked, and Glaive and Gabion barked confusedly on the other side of a wall of trampling feet and swirling skirts, Aurélie clung on to the miller, forcing him backwards, and Brind was able to wriggle free.

From his vantage point on the hay wagon that was his stage at the other end of the square, Brother Rohan couldn't see the cause of the distraction and was more than a little peeved at being suddenly ignored when in full flow. But as the crowd in the far corner thinned and then his entire audience began to funnel excitedly out of the square, he saw Lifford. The miller was brandishing his quarterstaff and running, almost skipping, towards the wagon. He seemed deliriously happy.

'Hue and cry, Brother!' he shouted. 'Hue and cry!'

Brind and Aurélie dodged round corner after corner. Glaive, at their heels, lost his footing at one sharp turn and crashed into the flimsy house wall opposite, provoking an angry shout and the sudden crying of a baby somewhere within, but the fugitives ran on. Gabion dodged in and out between them, barking excitedly. He enjoyed being chased as much as he enjoyed chasing. He couldn't be expected to understand what being caught on this occasion would mean.

Aurélie was trying desperately to remember the way back to the bridge, but even she, born and brought up in a town, was becoming confused by the patternless labyrinth of streets. She pushed at a gate that looked as if it might lead into a yard where they could hide, but it was bolted, just as it had been when she'd tried the same gate minutes earlier. She ran straight through a stall stacked with pots and pans and pewter mugs, sending them clattering and spinning to the ground. Seconds later the pursuing mob trod them flat. Then it tore through a draper's shop, rampaging among the hangings and rolls of cloth, in case the Devil's brood had gone to ground, while the shopkeeper's wife stood, tearfully begging them to stop. Aurélie could hear the wild destruction close behind them and dreaded the moment when she could run no further.

It was Brind who recognized the church. They had seen its spire from the hill before they had come down to the town, and when they'd crossed the bridge it was close by, just two tunnel-like streets from the river's edge. Two tunnels. Brind could smell the river. The main mob was close behind and he could hear others shouting on either side, trying to cut off the fugitives' escape. But if he and Aurélie could get to the bridge first, they would be free. No matter how many men and sticks and dogs the holy man and the miller sent after them into the forest, Brind would find a safe place for Aurélie. The forest was his territory.

A square of grey daylight appeared before the dog boy and he sprinted towards it, then somersaulted and sprawled heavily in the mud. Before he could comprehend that he'd been tripped, Aurélie and the hounds were in a heap on top of him.

Lifford, crouching hidden at the final corner, had brought them down, his quarterstaff held low across the alleyway like a tripwire. He straightened up now and stood back, laughing, as the mob spilled out of its burrow and swallowed up the Devil's brood.

Even Glaive's ferocious power couldn't save them. The mob had brought hurdles and surrounded the mighty mastiff and the black hellhound with these wicker shields, forcing the dogs back and back into the alleyway, and trapping them there, tight against a wall, while Brind and Aurélie were held on the ground by a dozen rough and willing hands.

Then more hurdles were brought and the two prisoners were hoisted on to them, tied down and carried shoulder-high, back through the streets to the market square. The mob danced and shouted alongside, occasional brave souls darting forward to pinch or poke the now helpless agents of the Devil. Brind jerked his head from side to side, instinctively trying to avoid these petty cruelties, but Aurélie stared steadfastly up at the eaves of the passing houses, and dreamed of revenge.

Lifford led the procession, strutting like a fighting cock. And when he reached Brother Rohan's wagon, he clambered nimbly aboard without being invited, standing as an equal beside the friar, as the market square filled again with excited townsfolk, and Brind and Aurélie were borne forward in triumph.

'Shall we burn them now?' asked Lifford eagerly.

Brother Rohan raised his hand slightly, a calm, checking, authoritative gesture. He didn't intend to allow this bumptious little peasant to force the pace. There were credit and gratitude, not to mention awe, to be bestowed first. And Brother Rohan was the rightful recipient.

The hurdle bearers had arrived in front of the wagon now. Brother Rohan gave them a nod and beckoned briefly, and Brind felt himself lurch and sway, and saw the sky spin as his hurdle was manhandled up on to the wagon. Aurélie's followed, and a great howl erupted as the two hurdles were propped and held upright, so that the prisoners tied to them were displayed to the seething crowd. Brind could hear another howl. Distant, helpless. Glaive in distress.

Brother Rohan spread his hands, palms down, as if smoothing a crumpled cloth, and the crowd became quiet.

'Brothers and sisters in God.' The friar paused, then indicated Brind and Aurélie. 'The Devil is thwarted. You are delivered from the jaws of death!'

The crowd roared again and surged forward, surrounding the wagon, arms outstretched to the holy man who so swiftly, so miraculously, had identified the enemy in their midst.

But as the general cry of relief subsided, a single voice, clear and strong, filled the air.

'How do we know?'

The question hung there, not aggressive, but demanding an answer, as heads turned, and

Brother Rohan scanned the crowd. A weather-beaten man with thin hair and a blue tunic was moving towards him.

'How do we know?' he repeated, then continued respectfully. 'Forgive me, Brother. You and your able assistant have served us well, but before we do what must be done, should there not be proof?'

'They killed the lady of the manor at Dowe,' cried Lifford hotly. 'And many others there. What more proof d'you want?'

The miller's question was echoed by many in the crowd, but the man in the blue tunic hoisted himself easily on to the wagon. He fixed his grey eyes briefly on Brind and Aurélie, and gave them an almost imperceptible shake of the head before turning and addressing those below rather than Lifford.

'Should we not put them to the test? If they are creatures of the Devil, it will become clear. If they are not, then we will know the town is not yet safe.'

He looked past Lifford at Brother Rohan.

'Put them to the test.'

It was a challenge, almost an order.

'The test, the test!' the crowd began to shout, and Brother Rohan felt his authority being eroded. Lifford looked ready to knock the man from the wagon, but it was too late for that. The sheeplike mob was with the newcomer now. It wanted the test. It wanted entertainment. Brother Rohan would have to indulge it or risk being, literally, overturned. Well, let the simple creatures have their fun. The end result would be the same: death of the Devil's brood.

'Of course I shall test them,' cried Brother Rohan, stepping in front of the man, his arms raised. 'That was always my intention.'

Lifford glowered and dug frustratedly at the floor of the wagon with his staff. Brother Rohan ignored him, but before he could continue, the newcomer addressed the crowd for him.

'Which ordeal do you wish them put to? Needles?'

The question provoked a cacophony of conflicting shouts, but gradually a call of agreement became dominant.

'Yes, needles! Needles! Needles!'

Then the crowd's united cry changed to noisy delight, and Brother Rohan turned to find that the man had taken a long steel pin from his tunic and was holding it high. The friar held out his hand, but the man moved straight towards Aurélie and leaned over her, with the pin poised.

Aurélie's mouth was dry. She was fearful and confused. She had recognized the man as he'd climbed on to the wagon and he clearly had recognized Aurélie and Brind. He was the merchant, the cheerful, garrulous man who had brought the cloth of gold to Dowe Manor. But now, instead of speaking for them, he'd become the friar's cruel accomplice. For Aurélie understood well enough what the test involved, understood that she would be pricked all over until a place that felt no pain was found. That place was the Devil's mark. The proof that she was a witch. She stared defiantly into the treacherous grey eyes and waited.

The crowd held its breath as the long steel pin flashed down but, astonishingly, Aurélie experienced nothing. More astonishingly still, the merchant mouthed silently at her as he struck.

'Scream.'

Aurélie screamed and, as the merchant methodically drove the pin at her arms and legs and back, she screamed again and again, even though each thrust inflicted less pain than the nip of a red ant.

'I know you are innocent,' whispered the merchant. 'Whatever brings the plague, I've seen enough on my travels to know it's not children . . .'

At each cry from the wagon, the spectators groaned in disappointment and, when the examiner eventually turned from Aurélie and addressed them again, they could only acquiesce.

'This girl is entirely human,' he exclaimed. 'She hurts, she bleeds. No part of her belongs to the Devil.'

'Then she is possessed by a demon and must be saved from it!'

Brother Rohan's voice was suddenly sharp and angry. He suspected sleight of hand by the interfering blue tunic and snatched the steel pin from him.

'*I* shall test the dog boy!'

And he drove the pin with all his strength and righteous anger into Brind's shoulder.

Nothing happened. The dog boy neither flinched nor cried out. Brother Rohan stepped back, momentarily shocked, leaving the steel pin upright, a finger's length deep in Brind's unfeeling flesh.

The crowd gasped. Aurélie strained her head towards the dog boy.

'Scream!' she hissed. 'Brind, scream, scream!'

But the bewildered dog boy felt no pain so he made no noise. The pin was lodged in the one nerveless part of his anatomy: where his arm had been almost pulled from its socket at the battle of Crécy. The shoulder joint had healed, but the feeling in it had been lost. Brother Rohan's luck had changed dramatically.

'See the insensible spot!' he proclaimed.

The mob was his again, spellbound. He placed his finger on the head of the long steel pin and beamed triumphantly at the blue tunic.

'The Devil's mark!'

A rumble of thunder overhead gave pleasing emphasis to his words and was echoed by a deep, vindictive snarl from his audience.

'One blow is not enough!' shouted the merchant, recovering from his own amazement, and he moved swiftly forward to ease the pin gently from Brind's shoulder.

But one blow, such a singular, awe-inspiring blow, was more than enough for the crowd. All eyes, all loathing, were now focused on the strange dog boy, the proven agent of the Devil. The plague bringer. And the sudden rain, which developed quickly into a hammering downpour, did nothing to damp down the growing, hate-filled tumult around the wagon.

Lifford shoved the merchant roughly away and hauled the hurdle with Brind lashed to it towards the wagon's side, where eager hands waited to take it. He was in a hurry now. The rain was cheating him of a bonfire, but there were other ways of cleansing the world, as Brother Rohan put it.

Aurélie twisted her wrists violently against the cords that bound her to the second hurdle. The woven willow creaked as she strained and she sensed that the hurdle itself might break if she could wrench it hard enough. She looked pleadingly towards the merchant. But Brother Rohan had not forgotten Aurélie. Suddenly he was in front of her, the rain bouncing off his smooth, glistening head.

'See how the demon within her struggles,' he said.

Four men had climbed on to the wagon at his bidding and now lifted the hurdle. The holy man's face loomed close over Aurélie's.

'We shall see if the saints can draw it from you.' He turned and shouted an order. 'Take her to the church!'

And the merchant could only watch helplessly, outnumbered by two hundred to one, as the children from Dowe Manor were carried to their separate fates.

The market square had quickly become a quagmire, and Brind's hurdle bearers slipped and slithered under their load. When one of them fell, the hurdle fell too, and Brind was spattered with mud as the nearest townsfolk squealed and scrambled fearfully away from him. But he was quickly hoisted up again and his bearers stumbled on.

Brind had lost sight of Aurélie as he was removed from the wagon. He hadn't understood the test, but knew that only he had failed it. He alone was being sent away, as Sir Edmund had sent him away. Taken from the town because the people thought he was the plague bringer after all, to be deposited deep in the forest, where he could do no harm. Confusion swamped him. Had Aurélie been wrong about the plague village? Was she safe? Could she get to Garwood without him? And there was another, equally deep anxiety: the dogs. Brind could no longer hear Glaive calling. Was he still alive? Had he escaped? How would Gabion survive?

The dog boy turned his head, recognizing the now-familiar tunnels. He was definitely being taken towards the bridge, towards the forest. Ahead of him, Lifford paced sure-footedly through the oozing mud and rivulets. Brind thought the town poorly constructed. No animal would dig a burrow that so quickly filled with water.

The mob was still with him, slopping along in silence now, all heads bowed under the deluge but determined to be present at the end. Brind wondered if he was to be accompanied like this all the way into the forest, but then he saw another crowd, already assembled on the bridge ahead of him. Waiting. And when those closest stood aside, he saw Glaive and Gabion.

The hounds were imprisoned in a rough wooden cage. Bloodied, despite the washing rain, and deeply subdued. On sight of Brind, they struggled to their feet and Glaive managed a low bark. But Brind's relief on seeing the dogs alive became confusion as he was dropped on the ground, and the cords around his wrists and ankles were cut, freeing him from the hurdle. Was he being released here? Simply sent on his way with his dogs, rather than forcibly carried further?

Brind was pulled to his feet and the saturated mob pressed closer, penning him in, those at the rear pushing and craning for a better view. The way across the bridge was completely blocked. And there was no way back. Only the parapet on the downstream side of the bridge was clear, and beyond that the swollen river tumbled and roared. Brind could hear and feel the bangs and scrapes as fallen trees from upstream collided with the bridge piers before being swept through.

Then Lifford's hand was on the dog boy's neck, thrusting him forward and down into the cage with the dogs. Brind was forced inside and the small sliding door dropped shut behind him. He tried to look round, to see if a wagon was being brought to carry the cage away from the town, but there was no room for him to turn. He was trapped on all fours, with Glaive and Gabion. And the stones. Brind hadn't noticed the stones before and didn't understand their purpose.

Glaive and Gabion were panting, lost and afraid. Glaive licked Brind's face, and Brind put his arm around the great dog's neck, then hung on when suddenly the cage was heaved into the air by half a dozen men and lowered on to the parapet.

As the cage stood lodged precariously above the

swirling brown water, the rain began to ease and the sun came out. Brind knew there would be a rainbow somewhere, though he couldn't move to see it. But he could see Brother Rohan. The friar had emerged from the crowd and was chanting in a language that Brind didn't understand.

As he came close, the holy man smiled and raised his arms before the dog boy. Then he turned and addressed the crowd, modestly containing his jubilation.

'So are the fires of Hell extinguished!' he cried.

And Lifford used his quarterstaff to lever the cage into the river.

5

Saint Tresoria

Brind should have drowned. That was the intention. The certainty. The Devil's boy and his black hellhound and his menacing guardian, the great mastiff, would all perish.

As the cage toppled from the parapet, the crowd rushed forward. Many were in time to see it hit the water and disappear; all could hear the heavy, satisfying splash above the noise of the continual torrent.

The cage would have sunk instantly even without its weighting of stones, but Brother Rohan had left nothing to chance. There was no escape. Another victory over the Devil had finally been secured.

The girl remained to be dealt with but, notwithstanding his suspicions of her testing with the steel pin, Brother Rohan was now in benevolent mood. He was prepared to give her the benefit of the doubt. If she were merely possessed by a demon, rather than having made a full compact with the Devil, he would cure the affliction. Possibly even take the girl with him on his further travels, to be displayed as an example of his power to overcome evil. Like a holy relic, only better. Brother Rohan warmed to the idea. He graciously accepted the reverential thanks of the crowd for a few minutes longer, piously declined the offer of being carried, then ploughed his way briskly back into the town through the stinking mire.

But Brind was not dead.

If the river had been its normal placid self, the cage would simply have settled on the bottom and its occupants' end would have been swift. But after months of rain, the waters surging between the narrow piers had formed a constant maelstrom below the bridge, a whirlpool that gouged the river bed and sucked and snatched at every branch, log and dead cow that came plunging through, churning them over, throwing them back time and again, before finally releasing them to race on towards the distant sea.

Heavy though it was, the cage was dragged into this barging underwater dance, and as Brind clung to the bars, terrified, eyes and mouth tight shut, ears full of thundering water, the roof of the cage was struck a crushing blow by a great submerged tree trunk. Instantly the bars gave way, and Brind was torn out and tossed among the spinning debris, before the back-current forced him up from the depths beneath the bridge, into air and light and a moment's chance of survival.

The dog boy instinctively threw up his hand, and his fingers touched a flimsy branch, part of a tree snagged horizontally between the piers. He grabbed the branch, but the handhold moved under his weight, and the perverse current immediately strained to drag him under again. Brind flailed with his other arm and felt it strike a thicker part of the tree. He kicked desperately and, as his first hand lost its grip, he managed to crook his other arm over the trunk. The tree slid again, alarmingly, but then stuck fast. Brind held on, summoning the last of his strength, then flung his first arm over the trunk as well and inched his way along the slippery wood to where the tree's roots were wedged against the timbers of the bridge. He paused again to recover, then hauled himself up and out of the water and crouched, shivering on the tree trunk, like a sickly water rat.

The river hurtled deafeningly past beneath him. And directly above, hidden from his sight as he was from theirs, the last townsfolk dragged their eyes away from what they contentedly supposed to be the watery tomb of the Devil's boy and made their way home.

But soon Brind's heart became as cold as his

aching arms, for there was no sign of Glaive or Gabion.

The spiral staircase was making Aurélie dizzy. Her shoulder brushed continually against its rough, cold stone, and as the turns became tighter, the flickering rushlight behind her was repeatedly blocked out, so that she was stepping down into total darkness.

She missed her footing and fell, but someone behind quickly pulled her up again, and echoing voices urged her on. Nervous voices. For her captors were afraid of the place they were entering.

At last, Aurélie felt a level floor of slippery flagstones beneath her feet, and when the rush-lights emerged from the staircase after her, she could see a low, vaulted ceiling, and stone walls, greened and glistening with water. And recesses in the walls, heaped with bones. Human bones. Some complete skeletons, mostly not.

In the centre of the floor stood a huge stone casket, longer than a man and waist-high. Aurélie's escort paused, glancing at the evidence of mortality all around them, and looking at each other uncertainly, none willing to make the next move.

Then another footfall became audible on the stairs: the slapping of sandals. And a waft of rose water, pungent in the damp, still air, preceded Brother Rohan into the crypt. He had washed the mud from his feet and legs and re-anointed himself. Exorcism was delicate work and the holy man preferred to be bodily prepared. Aurélie returned his gaze but not his beatific smile.

'So, my child,' he said. 'It is time for you to be left in peace a short while, so that the piety of the blessed martyr may prepare you for a return to grace.'

He spoke quietly but his voice boomed around the windowless walls. Then, at a nod from the friar, two townsmen began to move the lid of the great casket.

The scraping of stone on stone reverberated shrilly and set Aurélie's teeth on edge. And although the crypt was clammily cold, she began to sweat. The inside of the casket gaped before her. There was something inside, motionless and dimly white. Aurélie stiffened as hands gripped her arms again. She wanted to shout and fight, but her tongue and limbs refused, and she remained voiceless and rigid as she was hoisted up and lowered into the casket.

Brother Rohan continued to nod, and the last thing Aurélie saw as the casket lid was dragged back into place above her head was his face beaming down at her, like a full moon in the rushlight.

Aurélie sat quite still. She could see nothing, hear nothing. The floor of the casket felt lumpy beneath her, and when she did risk moving her legs something around and beneath them moved too.

Aurélie didn't move again for a long while. But, at length, she began to talk to herself, speaking out loud, berating herself for her cowardice, calling herself a mouse, a rabbit, a milksop, a disgrace to French womanhood, when she knew, yes, *knew* that all she was sharing this stupid stone box with was a few bones. All crypts contained bones. That was the purpose of a crypt. It was a place to put bodies and bodies wasted away and left bones. It was natural. Harmless. People could hurt you, their bones could not. There was absolutely no reason to be scared of bones, even when you were shut in a coffin with them. But when her twitching fingers lodged themselves in the eye sockets of a skull, Aurélie forgot that she was a disgrace to French womanhood and fainted.

Brind stayed beneath the bridge until dark. He had moved from the tree trunk and perched uncomfortably among its roots. Then, when the branches had eventually snapped and the whole tree had been wrenched away by the river, he had found a niche in the timber supports that rose to the parapet. Now he climbed slowly upwards, away from the cold of his cramped hiding place, into an airless night, lit by glimmering distant lightning.

In the long hours since the river had spat him out, Brind had come to terms with the fact that the people of the town had wanted to kill him. Not send or carry away. Kill. Kill the plague bringer. He knew he must remain out of sight, yet he was reluctant simply to cross the now-empty bridge and disappear into the forest. He wanted to see the river's edge in daylight, to search the inundated meadows and reed beds for Glaive and Gabion. He expected to find them drowned, but he wanted to find them.

And then he would try to find Aurélie. He had made up his mind on that too. He couldn't understand why, if Aurélie was wrong and everyone else was right, she hadn't been struck down by the plague, through contact with him, but it was a fact he couldn't ignore. She trusted him with her life. His duty was to Aurélie as much as to Sir Edmund.

At the town end of the bridge, a tall wooden building leaned out over the river, as if it were about to fall in. It smelt of cow and horse, and, as Brind crept towards it, the smell became so strong and putrid that he hesitated before seeking shelter inside. But he was chilled to the marrow, and the approaching thunder made up his mind.

Decrepit gates gave access to a yard, and the source of the stench: pile upon pile of animal hides, waiting too long to be cleaned and decomposing rapidly.

A low black tide ebbed from the skins as Brind approached. He had disturbed the rats. And he met more again as he clambered into the building itself. But the dog boy was not afraid of rats, and ignored them as they retreated unhurriedly and watched him from their secret places.

It was comfortingly warm in here and the smell was different, more bearable than outside. A strong, sharp odour rose from great round tubs of liquid and cut through the sickening reek of the hides. More skins were pegged on ropes close by. Cleaner, softer to the touch and easier on the nose. Stroking their smoothness, Brind recognized leather in the making. Sir Edmund occasionally sent cow hides to what he called a tannery. This must be such a place. Brind thought of the cow in the church, its diseased hide already peeling from its carcass, and he shrank back towards the sharp-smelling tubs. The floor was relatively dry and there was room to lie down on it. He curled up with his back against one of the tubs and fell swiftly into exhausted sleep, while the thundery rain renewed its assault on the town outside.

*

Aurélie awoke to the sound of the sky falling in. Then she realized that the casket lid was being rumbled open above her head. She gulped in air, for there was none left inside the sealed stone box, and the doze she was now rousing from had been more the start of a final unconsciousness than slumber. Desperately, she composed herself.

During the brief wakeful period between her faint and the suffocating drowsiness that had later overwhelmed her, Aurélie had tried to understand what would be expected of her if she lived. She had decided that she knew, and now she had to be ready to play her part.

'Is she alive?'

Aurélie heard Brother Rohan's hushed enquiry.

'If I am not,' she said, in a wondering, drowsy voice of childlike contentment, 'then I am in Heaven.'

Brother Rohan almost purred.

'See how she is soothed,' he whispered, in awe of the power of holy bones, and of himself for having prescribed so effective a cure. 'Lift her out. Gently. Gently . . .'

His order was obeyed, and Aurélie meekly allowed herself to be helped up and then arranged on the floor of the crypt, her back resting against the casket.

'Water,' commanded the friar, holding out his hand as he knelt in front of Aurélie. And when the jug was passed to him, he offered it to Aurélie as if presenting a gift, and supported the weight of it in his own hands as she took it unsteadily and drank.

Brother Rohan gazed searchingly at the girl when she had finished. Her shrewish little face, paler than ever in the feeble rushlight, seemed to have softened markedly. Even the eyes, formerly glinting with defiance and ill intent, had a calm, almost angelic lustre to them.

'My child,' said the holy man gravely. 'I do not expect you to understand the blessing that has been bestowed on you. You are but an ignorant French girl and many of your kind fall prey to the demons of Hell. Demons that crawl from that foul place in search of the unwary. Only be grateful that the demon that has occupied your body, and directed your acts for so long, has been put to flight. Bless and thank the bones of Saint Tresoria, in whose presence evil can only perish.'

'I do,' gasped Aurélie. 'But I thank you more, Father.' She grasped his hand with all the tremulous humility that she could muster. 'For it is you who has *truly* saved me.'

Brother Rohan was deeply gratified. Occasions such as this made all the hardships of life as a preaching friar worthwhile. Retrieving souls from the Devil was only marginally less satisfying than burning or drowning those who were proven to be beyond help. He crossed himself and began a long prayer in Latin.

Aurélie closed her hands and eyes and waited respectfully; and she didn't flinch when the friar's finger touched her bowed forehead and made the sign of the cross on it. Then she heard him stand up and opened her eyes to see him leaning over the casket rim.

When Brother Rohan knelt down again, he seemed almost in a trance, and was clutching something that he'd taken from the casket. He held it up to Aurélie as he spoke in a hushed voice.

'Seal your salvation,' he said. 'Kiss the skull of Saint Tresoria.'

And after a moment's panicked hesitation that the friar didn't notice, Aurélie kissed the crumbling, dusty skull as if it were the sweetest thing she had ever put to her lips.

She hoped St Tresoria would understand, and forgive her nausea.

The gates of the tannery creaked as they were dragged open through the gritty mud of the yard. And the wooden stairs creaked too as unwilling feet trudged up them into the lopsided building. There was a damp stain of river water beside one of the tubs, but in the gloomy dawn of another day's work, none of the tanners noticed it. Brind, dried, warmed and rested, was long gone.

Downstream from the town, the overfed river had swollen into a lake. The current was slacker here and the wreckage from upstream mostly came to rest on the grassy shores, or collected like an ever-building dam at the lower end, where the stream narrowed and quickened again.

Brind made his way watchfully along the water's edge, the swampy ground closing over his feet. The sun had risen but the sky was bruised dark purple with cloud. The colour reminded the dog boy of the plague and he kept his eyes on the water. His hopes rose when he found what he thought were some bars from the shattered cage, but sank at the sight of every bloated animal corpse grounded in the shallows.

Eventually Brind reached the cluttered log jam beyond which the river, cleansed of debris, rushed on its way. The jumble of branches, trunks and splintered planks presented an obstacle but also the only way across the water, and Brind needed to investigate the far bank of the lake before accepting the inevitable.

He clambered on to the closest branches, but soon found his natural bridge treacherous, for although locked together, the mangled trees were still afloat and Brind's weight threatened to free them. The dog boy moved as lightly and swiftly as he could, and was so intent on reaching the other side before he was washed away that he almost missed the upturned boat.

In the very middle, where the current was still strong, a small punt had fetched up against the tangled barrier and then been partly hidden by later flotsam. Wedged as it was, it formed a broad shield, deflecting the rushing water.

Brind's foot was on the boat when he felt rather than heard something beneath it. A feeble scratching. And then, as the dog boy's closeness was scented, a desperate whine of recognition.

Brind grabbed and heaved at the top edge of the boat, levering it over with no thought of the consequences for himself. He was rewarded with a glimpse of two bedraggled mastiffs, cowering on a platform of matted vegetation, before everything beneath and around him collapsed, and he and the dogs were caught in the watery avalanche.

As he surfaced, Brind cracked his head against the punt. The boat was upside down and too broad and slippery to heave himself on to. He clung to its side with his fingernails and looked desperately round for Glaive and Gabion. They were close by, powerless but with noses above the water, and Brind saw them before his eyes and mouth filled with mud as the current pushed him to the silted bank and drove the punt to a halt on top of him.

By the time the dog boy had heaved and

wriggled his way clear, and stood, blinded and coughing, waist-deep beneath the overhanging trees, Glaive and Gabion also had mud around their feet. Glaive barked and Brind stumbled towards the sound, hands outstretched until he felt the familiar fur beneath his fingers, and grabbed both dogs by the scruff of the neck to drag them step by step from the cloying silt.

When the water was below his knees, Brind let go and splashed his face until he could see, then scrambled out and threw himself down among the ground elder; and the dogs lolloped after him, barking and drenching him again as they shook themselves, before pouncing to lick the last of the mud from his nose and ears.

The chain came as a shock. Aurélie had thought she'd done the hard part in convincing Brother Rohan that she was cured. Saved. Once she had been led from the crypt below the church, it would be easy to just slip away. Disappear around a corner and leave the smug, odious, fanatical friar behind forever. But no. He had held her arm tightly as they climbed the spiral staircase, and he continued to hold it tightly as they emerged into the drizzling greyness that passed for daylight.

The blacksmith had been surprised to receive such visitors, but was obsequious to the point of grovelling and made no charge for the fine-link

94

steel. He had even helped Brother Rohan attach the chain to Aurélie's wrist. And then she had been paraded in the marketplace like a dancing bear, a freak.

The townsfolk had fallen to their knees amid the cabbage leaves and mud, and blessed the holy man for drawing the demon from the sweet girl whom they'd known all along wasn't really a witch.

Clearly, it was the dog boy and his hellhounds who were the true agents of the Devil, and Brother Rohan had destroyed them. The town was safe. It thanked the friar again and again and eventually showed its gratitude in the way he liked best, by feeding him.

So Aurélie was forced to sit demurely beside Brother Rohan while he devoured an eel pie, two chickens and a swan. It didn't seem to occur to the town or its honoured guest that the chained but demon-free girl was also hungry.

On the second day of feasting, a kitchen boy considerately scraped the remains of a dish of boar's trotters in her lap. And on the third, by which time even the wealthy burgesses of Horsham had begun to wonder how the next meal was to be paid for, Aurélie had her first taste of peacock, a dish, Brother Rohan had hinted repeatedly, that he adored above all meats. There was little left by the time it reached Aurélie, but at least when eating she didn't have to maintain the fixed ethereal smile of a newborn angel.

On the fourth day, with Lifford making everlouder noises about the need to seek out the Devil elsewhere, Brother Rohan finally bade Horsham a gracious farewell. The groom on whose back he stood in order to mount his horse regarded himself as highly favoured. And, as Brother Rohan rode out, with Aurélie's chain secured to his saddlebow, every man, woman and child tossed flowers and appreciation in the holy man's path. All except the family tossing with a sudden fever in the hovel behind the draper's shop. And the boy, crouched watching in the flooded hazel copse beyond the bridge, his hands on the muzzles of two half-submerged dogs.

Lifford rode in silence, which was normal, but he was simmering with more than his usual anger and occasionally gave vent to his frustration by jabbing Aurélie in the back with his quarterstaff. The girl's presence was irritating and the way she kept tripping over tree roots intensely so. Lifford didn't trust Aurélie. Didn't believe in her new angelic self. She was a witch and should have burned. That was why he had left home: to hunt down and burn witches; not amble about the countryside, listening to the preening friar's sermons and watching him eat.

Brother Rohan was blithely unaware of the miller's resentment. He had no misgivings at all about Aurélie's true nature or his own judgement, and had convinced himself that even if the man in the blue tunic hadn't intervened, he would have come to the same conclusion. The girl had been savable and he had saved her. The chain by which he led her was simply a precaution, not against innate wilfulness on Aurélie's part, but against further attempts by the Devil to lead her astray. Patients were always most vulnerable immediately after they had been cured.

If Brother Rohan had been truly able to see into Aurélie's heart, he would have been less complacent. But the hostility that burned inside her was powerless and, unlike Lifford, she had no outlet for it. Whenever she felt the sharp jab of the staff in her back, she wanted to whirl round and drag the miller from his horse, but it would be a brief, empty victory, even if she could manage it. She was a prisoner. The chain that kept her so was light, almost elegant, yet with every step it seemed heavier, uglier, more humiliating.

Aurélie tried hard to think of other things, in particular the merchant who had deceived Brother Rohan with his steel pin. Perhaps he would try again and even now was watching, slipping through the trees, about to burst upon them. He would skewer Brother Rohan and Lifford on the quarterstaff, like a hog and a quail on the same spit, and then whisk Aurélie away to Garwood, with a cloak of cloth of gold around her shoulders.

But the beautiful daydream was too fragile to keep out thoughts of Brind and Gabion and Glaive. For Aurélie had learned enough from the townsfolk's prattle when they had been worshipping and feasting the friar to realize that Brind was dead. Caged and drowned with his dogs. And the next time she was butted in the back, her anger exploded.

Aurélie spun round and grabbed at the tormenting quarterstaff, but immediately was yanked from her feet, because although she had stopped walking, Brother Rohan's horse, to which her chain was attached, had not. Instead of pulling Lifford down, Aurélie herself was tumbled along the ground away from him. She rolled on to her front and tried to regain her footing, but, despite Lifford's roar of laughter, Brother Rohan seemed oblivious to her sudden fall from grace. Indeed, he was digging his heels into the old horse's flanks, urging it on faster, and Aurélie had to cling to the chain with her free hand to prevent her arm being pulled off. Stones in the rough track gouged her knees, then the horse veered sideways and Aurélie was dragged to a merciful halt just short of a spiteful-looking clump of thistles.

'You're a fool, Brother,' jeered Lifford, as he

brought his horse up behind Aurélie and pushed her over again as she tried to stand up. 'She's no more saved than the Devil himself.'

But the friar still wasn't listening. He had dismounted and was walking the few paces towards a small shelter, a piece of canvas tied between two saplings. Beyond it, a tethered packhorse had already turned its back incuriously and resumed grazing. Inside the shelter lay a man curled under a blanket. Brother Rohan glanced only briefly towards him and instead crouched before what appeared to Aurélie to be more canvas. But even from the track the friar had seen something beneath it: the reluctant sunshine had illuminated thread of gold.

As Aurélie edged as close as the chain would allow her, she saw that the canvas on the ground was the untied covering of a pack. The man lying in the shelter still hadn't moved. Only a few strands of grey hair and part of his sleeved arm showed above the blanket. The sleeve was blue, the arm inside it stiff. Aurélie looked towards the packhorse and recognized the frayed ribbon, also blue, knotted in its mane. In a shocking, painful way her daydream had come partly true: this was the man who had tried to rescue her, who had saved her life in effect. But the rest of the dream would not be coming true. The merchant was dead.

Brother Rohan had not looked at the man

closely enough to recognize him: he had eyes only for the pack. There were two full rolls of cloth of gold, as well as furs, and as the friar greedily unravelled his find, Aurélie again remembered Lady Beatrice's delight on that golden day at Dowe.

She blinked away tears to find a perversion of the memory being enacted before her. Brother Rohan had wrapped a length of the rich cloth around his shoulders like a cape.

'You're not the Pope yet,' said Lifford.

Brother Rohan ignored the sarcasm, or was too lost in greed to notice it.

'Untether the packhorse,' he ordered.

'Untether it yourself,' replied the miller. Then he slid nimbly from the saddle and strode forward. 'In fact, if you're intent on taking what's not yours, we'll divide it. Now.'

'The man is dead,' said the friar, without looking up. He was repacking the cloth of gold, tucking it carefully inside the canvas. 'God did not give the world such beauty in order that it be wasted.'

'I said, we'll divide it.' Lifford was standing over him now. The tip of the quarterstaff missed the holy man's hand only narrowly as it jolted down on the canvas.

Brother Rohan looked up and smiled.

'If you wish.'

Lifford raised the staff and Brother Rohan

unfolded the pack, then unhurriedly separated the furs from the golden cloth.

'All the furs are yours,' said the friar.

'Furs make me sneeze, Brother,' replied the miller. 'Cloth of gold doesn't.'

There was a gleam in Lifford's eye. He was sick of the holy man and, although small in stature by comparison, was confident of his own physical superiority.

Brother Rohan paused, then shrugged matter-of-factly, piety forgotten. This was business.

'Very well, half the cloth of gold each.'

The staff jabbed down again and this time hit the friar's hand, hard.

'No, Brother,' said Lifford. 'You may have the furs. *I* shall take the cloth of gold. All of it.' He smiled. 'In fact, would I not be doing you a great service, given your holy vow of poverty, by leaving you with neither furs *nor* golden cloth? Perhaps then you would concentrate better on the task of killing witches.'

Lifford anticipated meek submission, even a craven blessing as he rode off laden with plunder. He did not anticipate the staff being whipped from under him and ending across his windpipe as he lay flat on his back, with the friar's full weight crushing the breath out of him.

'Do not instruct *me*, flour mite.'

Brother Rohan was breathing hard, close to

Lifford's astonished, bulging eyes. He pressed down on the staff and the miller gagged, his arms flailing helplessly, like the wings of a pinned moth.

Aurélie had been as unprepared as Lifford for the friar's sudden display of agile strength. She was even less prepared for the light touch on her shoulder and instant hand across her mouth to stifle any cry of surprise that might follow. Then she recognized the long, black nails and her shock was greater still. Brind was back from the dead.

The dog boy said nothing, glancing only briefly at the unequal struggle in the grass a few paces away, before ducking under Brother Rohan's horse. His fingers worked quickly at the buckle of the leather girth, and before Aurélie had understood what he was doing, she felt the steel chain slacken as the saddle slipped sideways towards her. The stolid old horse made no sound or movement as Brind pulled the unfastened saddle and girth from it and, with a swift nod at Aurélie, ran off with them into the trees, with Aurélie and chain still attached.

Lifford's florid face was changing colour. Brother Rohan had only to press for a few seconds longer and the miller would be dead. No great loss to the world. Quite the opposite. The friar was tempted. But he so loved the power of life and death that at the last moment he eased back. Lifford had been crushed, in every respect. It was enough.

'You may take your horse. You may take your staff. You may take yourself,' breathed the holy man. 'That is all.'

Then he withdrew the staff from across Lifford's throat and levered himself upright.

Lifford lay for some time, gulping and making unpleasant gurgling noises. When finally he had crawled weakly to his feet and on to his horse, he tried to curse the friar but the muscles in his throat wouldn't work. Brother Rohan tossed the quarterstaff to him dismissively and Lifford dropped it. Whereupon the friar picked it up, forced it beneath the straps of Lifford's saddlebag and slapped the horse's rump so that it bolted off towards the track with Lifford clinging precariously to its neck.

Only then did Brother Rohan turn towards his own horse and find it missing both a saddle and a French girl saved from the Devil.

6

The Nettle Bed

Brind gnawed at the saddlebow like a dog at a bone. Eventually he had chewed enough to weaken the pommel and tear it off so that he could release the knotted chain. The steel remained banded to Aurélie's wrist, but at least she would be able to move freely now.

'Thank you,' she said, and wound the chain around her arm as if it were an elaborate bangle, then smiled affectionately and gave a rueful shrug, very much aware of what Brind had suffered, even though he'd said nothing of it himself. 'Perhaps Horsham wasn't such a good idea after all.'

Brind put his finger to his lips. Glaive's body had tensed and, in the silence that the dog boy's look commanded, Aurélie finally heard hoof beats. Heavy, slow. Coming closer.

Brind crept away through the leaf litter towards the edge of the track and Aurélie followed. Gabion made to scamper after her but Glaive growled and Gabion sat down again.

Two horses came into view. On one was the merchant's pack of furs and cloth of gold, its canvas covering carefully secured. On the other, somewhat less secure without a saddle or stirrups, was Brother Rohan. He was concentrating too hard on staying upright to turn his head, but as the holy man jolted by Brind gripped Aurélie's arm firmly, sensing that she might fly out at him.

When the track was silent and empty again, Brind called softly to the dogs and beckoned Aurélie to follow. He was clearly eager to continue away from the town. Aurélie laid a hand on his arm.

'I'm sorry, Brind. There's something we have to do first.'

They buried the merchant as best·they could, wrapping him first in his canvas shelter, as a shroud. Aurélie looked from the plague-ridden corpse to the silent, sorrowful dog boy and knew that, despite the evidence of the stricken village, Brind was firmly back to blaming himself.

'Touch merchant's hand at Dowe,' he muttered, staring at the corners of canvas protruding beneath the scraped earth.

'Help with furs. Touch charcoal burner . . . Touch Lady Beatrice . . .'

'*I'm* not dead,' interrupted Aurélie, and she

grabbed his hand in case he had it in mind to run away again. 'Am I? *Am* I?'

Brind frowned and shook his head, but as if accepting a mystery rather than seizing hope.

'Well, why not, if you're the plague bringer?' demanded Aurélie.

She was bullying him: there was no time for melancholy resignation. Even the dogs looked contrite, as if they were included in the telling-off.

'Answer me. Why not?'

Brind said nothing, then gave an awkward shrug and looked away.

'Find Garwood,' he mumbled. 'Find Lady Alice.'

'Yes,' said Aurélie emphatically. 'That's more like it.'

Lifford had made a decision. There was too much treachery in the world: the country was full of thieving rogues. It was grievously unfair that a free man could not enjoy adventure without being throttled by a pot-bellied, shiny-pated bullfrog masquerading as a servant of God. The miller's career as a witch hunter had been, literally, strangled almost before it had begun. And any notion he had harboured of branching out on his own had been strangled with it. Without the unspeakable friar to give the enterprise authority, he was just an angry little man with a quarterstaff, charging around southern England on a red horse. In his heart, Lifford was not a bold spirit. He was a flour mite. He turned his horse for home.

Rain had returned to Dowe with a vengeance. As if it had moved away just long enough for the plague to pass through and was now impatient to inflict its own lower form of misery again.

The ditch on the hill was refilling as quickly as weary hands could empty it, mud and water combining in a continuous, inexorable slide over its dissolving rim. Soon there would be no ditch at all, nowhere for the pitiless rain to go, other than into the next field down the slope, and then the cottages below that, taking the remains of the unripened crop of wheat along with it. Even less food for the winter. Worse, even less shelter if the cottages were engulfed in a mudslide.

Sir Edmund dredged up another bucketful of yellow-grey sludge and heaved it out of the ditch. Behind and in front of him, the men and women from the cottages did the same. Four of them and their children. The only labouring families who had survived the plague and also remained at Dowe, instead of disappearing into the forest. The least Sir Edmund could do was to stand shoulder to shoulder with them. Feudal duty worked both ways. He felt better for having stirred himself, and the exhausting struggle stopped him thinking about Brind and Aurélie.

The heavy, saturated clay sucked at Sir Edmund's legs, binding him deep in the mud, like a tree stump, so that he had to dig himself out before he could resume the battle against the flood. As he worked, he prayed that the rain would stop. He had prayed a lot since the madness had left him. Mostly one simple, repeated, agonized prayer: that he might somehow be given the chance to undo the harm he had done.

A narrow blue line of sky appeared to the west and Sir Edmund willed it towards him. Even half an hour's respite from the downpour would be something. As he stood knee-deep in the mire, summoning up the strength to resume dredging, he saw a horseman silhouetted against the broadening band of blue, where the track to Dowe Manor rose briefly above the surrounding forest. The sun came out, blinding Sir Edmund, and he cursed it momentarily. He was apprehensive: his recent visitors were still on his mind. Had there been only one horseman on the ridge? He could see none now. Sir Edmund clambered out of the ditch and his mud-heavy feet slithered into a run.

Lifford hadn't intended to arrive from the west. It was a much longer way round, but after passing Horsham he'd become lost and spent several hours muttering oaths at himself for having simply followed Brother Rohan away from Dowe, instead of noting the route.

He had decided it would be wise to visit Sir Edmund first, rather than merely return to the mill and resume grinding corn as if nothing had happened. He was not a serf, but he depended on Sir Edmund for work. Besides, there was precious little corn to grind: the early crops had been disastrous.

The manor yard looked much the same as when he'd ridden away from it in such excitement. The excitement, like his throat, had been crushed and he didn't expect a warm welcome. He didn't get one. Sir Edmund marched into the yard, looking as if he'd rolled through a mud bath.

'Oh,' said the old knight. 'It's you.'

The scent of wild boar was suddenly strong in the beech wood and getting stronger, so Brind let the dogs follow it. He had no means of skinning or cooking meat, but if the dogs managed a kill, perhaps he and Aurélie could sell it, or exchange it for food.

Brind ran excitedly after the hounds, and for once was slow to pick up the sound of danger: horses' hooves, approaching fast. The horsemen were almost upon him. He called off the hounds with an urgent bark and Glaive responded instantly. But Gabion continued to dodge back and forth in the low undergrowth, oblivious to everything except the intoxicatingly close scent of wild boar. As Brind raced towards him, he barked excitedly, his tail thrashing, then yelped in hurt surprise as Brind dived on top of him, burying the dog's jaws in the beech mast.

Brind turned his head, frantically looking for Aurélie. She too had heard the horsemen now and was stumbling towards Brind as fast as she could. When she reached him, he pulled her down and dragged her with him as he crawled forward into a broad patch of brambles, burrowing into its face-scratching depths as if he were the quarry, going to earth. Brind pushed Gabion roughly ahead, then clamped the young dog's jaws tightly shut, stifling any sound, as the horsemen reined in close by.

'You've lost him, Goss,' laughed one of the hunters.

'*I've* lost him? You were in front. And you're the one who reckons he can scent like a dog.'

'While you merely smell like one.'

The laughter sounded almost directly above Brind. Up through the tracery of stems and thorns he could see the horses wheeling and then the glint of steel as the two riders clashed hunting spears in mock battle.

'Kendrick, he's here!'

Brind buried his head desperately in Gabion's

neck at the sudden shout, and the young hound scrabbled and writhed in front of him. Then something rougher than brambles rasped across Brind's hand, small sharp feet briefly trampled his back and a frightened wild boar broke cover, leaving his rank odour behind him.

With much shouting, the two hunters galloped off after their quarry, and when their noise had faded to nothing, Brind slowly backed out of the brambles, dragging Gabion with him. It took a while for Aurélie to extricate herself, the thorns tearing her dress in a most vexing way as she did so. When she finally emerged, Brind was growling angrily at Gabion, occasionally uttering short, sharp barks by way of emphasis. Glaive sat watching and seemed to nod sanctimoniously, which irritated Aurélie, but she felt the need to apologize nonetheless.

'I'm sorry,' she said. 'It's my fault he doesn't concentrate.'

'Yes,' said Brind, scowling at her with unexpected vehemence. 'Your fault.'

Aurélie was taken aback. Gabion's indiscipline could have cost them their liberty, perhaps their lives. But it hadn't. Brind pointed at the dogs and then at himself.

'Pack leader,' he said. 'Only one.'

'You've never made such a fuss before.'

Aurélie didn't want to sound petty, but she was

genuinely stung by the sudden criticism. Brind was leashing Gabion with his belt, as he'd done when they'd arrived at Horsham.

'Garwood,' he growled, thrusting the belt leash at Aurélie. 'Hold Gabion all the way.'

'Hold him yourself,' retorted Aurélie. 'You're the pack leader.'

And she stalked past the dog boy with her nose in the air.

'She's what!'

Sir Edmund had refound his temper as well as his wits.

'On a chain,' said Lifford. 'Brother Rohan drew the demon from her, or says he did, then led her away. On a chain.'

'What in Heaven's name for?' demanded Sir Edmund, as bewildered as he was outraged.

'To prove how clever he is,' said Lifford. His throat was hurting, but it was soothed by speaking against the bullfrog. 'I tried to stop him. Told him I'd been mistaken and he was mistaken too, but he wouldn't listen. He's a wicked man.'

'And Brind and the dogs?'

Lifford shrugged and stirred dirt on the floor with his quarterstaff.

'As I say, my lord, the friar's a wicked man.'

'What's happened to them!' roared Sir Edmund in his face.

Lifford blinked.

'The friar drowned them,' he said. 'In the river at Horsham. In a cage. Weighted with stones.'

His throat was feeling so much better. Sir Edmund stood very still, then prowled the kitchen for a full minute before speaking again, in a quiet, level voice.

'And where is the holy man leading Aurélie on this chain?'

'Away from Horsham, to the east.'

'When did he leave?'

'Two days ago.'

Sir Edmund prowled again, then stopped behind Lifford. The news of Brind had all but crushed the old knight's spirit under a new weight of guilt. But the miller's return offered a glimmer of hope in respect of Aurélie.

'You've always wanted to be a huntsman, isn't that right?'

'Me, my lord?' Lifford was startled.

'That's what you're forever whining on about, isn't it? How unfair it is that you're not allowed to hunt in my forest?'

Lifford wondered who'd been gossiping. Probably his wretched wife.

'Not at all, my lord. I'm very happy with my station in life.'

'Well, if you want to retain that station, *any* station, you'll lead me to the French girl. Now!'

Before Lifford could reply, Sir Edmund snatched the quarterstaff from the miller's hands and smashed it in half with Milda's meat cleaver. He tossed the two pieces on to the cooking fire. Lifford felt naked.

Sir Edmund strode briefly from the kitchen and returned with a much shorter stick, a whipstock.

'Here,' he said, thrusting it at Lifford. 'This is more your size. Muster the hounds.'

It wasn't what Lifford had bargained for. He felt out of his depth. Indeed, as the sea of baying hounds seethed around him, he feared he would fall from his horse and drown horribly. But Sir Edmund rode confidently among them, bawling unintelligibly and pointing them in the right direction, and Lifford actually felt a spurt of pride as he followed the raucous mastiffs out on to the track. He hoped his wife was watching.

This was the second time in little more than a week that the miller had left Dowe in pursuit of the French girl. Then she'd been a witch. Now she was a damsel in distress. Lifford still wasn't a knight, but he didn't mind that: if they found the friar, there would be no rules of honour to prevent him tearing the holy man limb from perfumed limb.

'Garwood Manor?' asked Aurélie. 'Do you know the way?'

The boy she was speaking to was younger than her but leaned on his stick like a thoughtful old man. The goats he was tending crowded round Aurélie and tried to eat the frayed hem of her dress.

'Away from the sun,' the boy said at last, and pointed.

The sun was setting, so he meant go east, and seemed certain enough of the direction, if not the distance, so Aurélie thanked him with a smile. The boy returned the smile and invited the travellers to come back to his mother's cottage and share supper. But Brind, who was standing apart, shook his head violently and tugged Glaive and Gabion away, and Aurélie followed the dog boy reluctantly, in silence.

It was not a comfortable silence. Aurélie was still smarting. Brind might be pack leader, but she most definitely was not part of the pack. It was true that she occasionally shouted at Brind, but that was for his own good. Not at all the same as being barked at for the behaviour of a dog. Aurélie was also cold and resented being denied the hospitality of the goatherd's family. Brind could have sat outside with his hands behind his back if he wanted to maunder on about plague-bringing. Now they would be bedding down, foodless, in some soggy, dripping hole in the ground. Again.

Brind did better than a dripping hole in the

ground, though not much. He found a forester's hut with a dripping hole in the roof. Also, after being gone a long time, he found food, returning with an armful of yellow bracket fungus. He broke off a layer and offered it to Aurélie. It glowed sulphurous in the twilight.

Aurélie should have been hungry, but she accepted the fungus only to show how gracious she was in the face of Brind's hurtful behaviour. And retreated with it to the darkest corner of the hut, where she nibbled half-heartedly at the bitter but tender flesh and let the surprising yellow juice trickle down her chin unlicked.

Perhaps she had simply eaten too much raw forest food in her adventures with Brind to be able to face any more. Perhaps it was the air in the hut, or lack of it, the vague smell of wild animal, that was making her gorge rise. Perhaps she just had a chill. Yes, a chill. That would explain the shivering.

When Brind noticed a rusty iron spike in the door post and, having managed to loosen and pull it out, used it to prise open the chained metal band on Aurélie's wrist, she barely managed a smile of thanks as she slid her arm free.

Brind looked disappointed and returned to the dogs, leaving the chain where it had fallen in a chinking heap. Aurélie pressed her back against the spider-infested wall, glad to be ignored, while the dog boy resumed tossing pale grey mushrooms for Glaive and Gabion to leap and snap at, then ate his way earnestly through the rest of the yellow fungus.

When she woke later in the night, Aurélie knew she was going to be sick. She lay sweating for a short time, while waves of nausea washed over her, then moved. She had to get outside. It would be awful to vomit here in the tiny hut. Disgusting, embarrassing. Aurélie tried to stand up, but she had a peculiar sense of spinning, even though she could see nothing, and then the nausea returned and she collapsed. Gabion and Glaive were both awake now, and Aurélie lay as still and quiet as she could, despite the violent shaking of her legs and arms, waiting until she heard the dogs settle. She didn't want Brind to wake: she could be sick without him. When all was still again, she crawled on her hands and knees out into the fresh air.

The violence of the vomiting, when finally she succumbed to it, frightened Aurélie. There could be nothing left inside her, but still she retched uncontrollably.

She rolled on to her back to let the night breeze cool her face, but instantly felt the gentle wind bite her like a wintry gale. So she rolled over again and dragged herself down through the ground ivy that covered the small hill in front of the hut, away from the spiders, away from Brind and the dogs, seeking privacy, warmth and, above all, relief. And eventually, still on all fours, delirious with fever, she scrabbled determinedly in a patch of nettles, ripping them up by the roots, convinced she was pulling back the coverlet of a welcoming bed; and then she curled herself up in the soft, loamy hollow that she had dug.

A band of mist lay low across the forest, its upper edge smooth and flat, as if planed level in the night; and as the mastiffs gambolled in the leaf litter, their damp bodies, like the ground itself, began to smoke in the orange warmth of the rising sun.

Brind wasn't watching the dogs. He stood outside the hut, peering into the mist. Perplexed. Where had Aurélie gone? Why had she gone? He knew she was still angry with him, despite being freed of the chain, and he hadn't known what else to do to make her smile again, but surely she wouldn't have just gone on to Garwood without him? Another, wilder fear assailed him for a moment: she'd left because he was the plague bringer and she was, after all, afraid to stay with him. Then Brind laughed at himself for being stupid. She must have simply woken up thirsty and gone to find fresh water. Or hungry and gone to find more fungus; though she hadn't seemed to like what he'd brought last night. She would be back soon.

But then Brind noticed the curious track through the ground ivy. As if something had been dragged away down the hill.

Aurélie had paid no great attention to the pimple on her shoulder when she'd first noticed it in the town. It had itched a bit, and its head had turned black instead of the usual red or yellow, but she was used to flea and lice and insect bites: they were part of living, especially in summer, and they were bound to be even more varied and vile here in the forest.

But the pimple had now grown into a kind of black bruise, not a healthy bruise but a raised bruise, full of pus. Aurélie wanted to brush it from her skin, as if it were some loathsome living thing that had settled on her, but she couldn't reach it, couldn't move her free hand across her body: her arms and neck had become rigid.

She was painfully aware that the sun had risen. It hurt her eyes. And as she struggled to turn her back to its glare, she realized that something was trapped under her arm. Beneath the shoulder on which the poisoned bruise sat.

Through her fever, she remembered climbing into bed. There must have been something in the bed. Perhaps Milda had put in a hot stone to warm it for her. Or a loaf, in case she became hungry. It felt small and hard, just like one of Milda's loaves. Caught under her arm. Aurélie couldn't reach her shoulder, but she could just reach her armpit. The loaf was still warm and wasn't so hard after all.

But the strange thing was, it was growing from her body.

7

Chanterelle

The hounds knew what they were looking for and Brind padded urgently behind them as they followed Aurélie's scent along the strange trail gouged through the forest floor. Brind had dismissed the idea that someone, or something, had entered the hut and dragged Aurélie away. It would have been impossible without waking the dogs. Nor was there anything in the hut that Aurélie, if she'd slipped away alone, could have dragged behind her. The only conclusion was that Aurélie had dragged herself. The hounds' call of discovery, when it came, made Brind run all the faster, and not just because he needed to quieten them for safety's sake. Glaive's voice was mournful and the dog boy was chilled by it. He had heard that sound before.

Aurélie was aware of the dogs. She felt their breath, she heard their voices. The breath was close on her neck, but the voices were far away. She tried to lift her head but had to let it drop again. It seemed to be splitting open and was best left where it was. Close in front of her glazed eyes, a beetle that had fallen from her hair struggled upwards again, clambering through the crushed nettles towards her nose. She was lying on her side in a tight ball, her hand still pressed inside her armpit. She knew that what she'd found there wasn't a loaf or a stone. She knew it was the plague. The fever had sweated all the tears out of her, so she couldn't cry, except inside.

Something heavy was resting on Aurélie's shoulder. The good shoulder, not the bad one. The bad one was buried beneath her. She was being moved. Rocked. She heard another dog's voice. Low and growling. Out of the corner of her eye, she could see the new dog's large paw on her shoulder.

Brind was trembling as he crouched in front of Aurélie. Shock. Fear. Guilt. Especially guilt. He had overcome all these to move within touching distance. What was left was a tenderness of such intensity that Brind forgot to breathe. Never had he seen Aurélie like this. Even their first meeting in France, when she had been so desolate, had turned into a fight. She would not be fighting now. She was helpless, lost and disfigured, as Lady Beatrice had been. And so fragile. Brind moved her gently, as he would a damaged bird, prising her clenched, terrified body from the ground and turning it to expose the hidden shoulder.

Just below the ragged seam, where her dress had been torn in the brambles, he saw the black mark. There was another blotch on her neck, but when he tried to lift her arm, she initially resisted. Still growling softly, he wiped the caked soil from her cheek and hair, then tried again. This time she let her arm be moved. And Brind was confronted with the monstrous black swelling that filled her armpit.

'Plague,' he murmured. But the hounds, who sat licking themselves behind him, were unconcerned now that Brind and Aurélie had been reunited.

The dog boy had no thought of saving Aurélie. Those that he had touched died. But he could and would ease the suffering he had finally brought upon her. He knew that bites, scratches, stings, even the touch of certain plants could cause swellings. Not just on humans but on dogs, cows, horses. And swellings often produced fever. If he could reduce Aurélie's fever, by bringing down the swelling, perhaps she could sleep peacefully. It was all he had to offer.

Brind had no knife or needle, so he went in search of briars and found a dog rose. Its blossom had been shredded by the rain, but its thorns were hard and sharp. And with one of these thorns,

Brind punctured the growth in Aurélie's armpit and squeezed the hot, putrid contents into the dirt.

Sir Edmund broke camp at sunrise. It had been hard to contain the hounds at night with no paddock fences, let alone a sleeping lodge. He had no food for them and little enough for himself and Lifford. The miller's eagerness to please, though, was startling. He had brought Sir Edmund water from the nearby stream before dawn and was now doing his best to supervise the pack as it splashed and rootled and chased around, picking up the myriad scents that lay heavy on the dew.

Sir Edmund had brought with him a scarf that Aurélie always wrapped around her neck when complaining of the unhealthy damp of the English winter. It was too soon to give it to the hounds yet and he was apprehensive that they might not pick up the scent when he did. If Brind and Glaive were here, it would be different. But Brind and Glaive were dead, and would never lead the hounds again. Sir Edmund was left with Lifford.

The old knight heaved himself stiffly into the saddle, wincing at the pain in his hips and knees. At least he and the miller were on horseback. Aurélie was apparently being led on foot. If they pushed on, they might overtake her tomorrow. He shouted at Lifford and the dogs, and rode away into the orange ball of sun.

Aurélie did sleep. Brind heaped bracken over her and, though they were wide awake and restless, made Glaive and Gabion lie close against her, to keep her warm. Then he crouched and waited, while the heavy sun crawled slowly across the forest.

By late afternoon, Aurélie still hadn't moved and Brind began to think that she had died. But when he crept forward and touched her nose, she twitched slightly. Brind sat down again and watched intently. He hardly dared let himself, but he began to hope. And when the sun set and night stole through the forest so that he could no longer see clearly, Brind moved closer to his patient, in order to hear any slight movement that she might make.

No dreams disturbed Aurélie, and when she opened her eyes she knew that she had done so, even though she could see more with them shut. Behind her eyelids, there were points of light, some of them coloured, red and green. Outside, there was only blackness. It was like being in the hut, though she knew that she wasn't. It was also like the kennel sleeping lodge at Dowe, with its smell of bracken and dog. But fresher. She breathed cool air, and coughed, and instantly there was movement and noise all around her. And although Aurélie still had no idea where she was, she knew with absolute clarity who was with her.

She raised her head and rejoiced in its hollow lightness. Her entire body felt hollow and light, as if a puff of wind would send her tumbling away. Everything still ached, and her life pulse seemed concentrated in her throbbing armpit, but the poisonous heat was gone and with it the wild imaginings of fever. She could move her hand and touch her forehead, and her forehead was cool and dry. She stretched out the hand and felt the dogs lick it, then another hand grasp it. Aurélie smiled, or tried to. She knew what she wanted to say and hoped the dog boy would hear her.

'Not plague bringer. Plague healer.'

She was rewarded with the sight of his sharp white teeth in the darkness, suddenly visible in a wide grin.

When daylight came again, Aurélie's appearance was disturbing. The dark patches on her neck and shoulder were already fading, but she looked as frail and skeletal as a fallen leaf. Brind feared she would break in his hands as he helped her to her feet. She had insisted on moving, but when they had laboriously followed a small muddy stream to its source, she accepted defeat and sagged among the ferns, her head bowed, while Brind scooped up spring water and held it to her lips.

Aurélie needed food and, leaving the dogs with her, Brind went hunting. He longed to find a honeycomb, but there were no bees. The only fungus he encountered was old and rotting, and the only berries were rose hips, their skin so discoloured and the seeds inside so hard and bitter that even Brind spat them out.

When he returned empty-handed, Aurélie was exactly where he'd left her, too listless to show disappointment at the lack of breakfast. She lay back on the ground while Brind hurried to a clump of hazel saplings close by and started tearing at their flimsy stems and branches. Aurélie could hear the ripping of ivy from tree trunks, and the snap and split of young wood, and eventually struggled up on an elbow to see what the dog boy was doing. He seemed to be making some kind of hurdle or raft with handles, the springy hazel stems tied together with thick tendrils of ivy and nightshade. Realization finally struck.

'No, Brind, don't be stupid. I can walk.'

To prove the point, she made a supreme effort and staggered to her feet. But she managed only a couple of steps towards him before having to grab the nearest tree to stop herself from keeling over.

'Brind, you can't drag me all the way to Garwood.'

Aurélie wasn't sure whether she was more upset

by the hardship the dog boy would be imposing on himself or the indignity of bumping along behind him. But when she tried to walk again she found she dared not let go of the tree, so she resignedly leaned against it until Brind had finished, then did as she was told and lay down on the makeshift litter, holding tight as Brind stepped between the handles and lifted them up, testing the balance.

Then, without warning, Brind barked at the dogs and jogged away, pulling the litter after him. Facing backwards, Aurélie nestled in her cradle of branches after the initial jolt, watching the twin furrows left by the litter uncoil in the leaf mould like endless identical serpents. And then she fell asleep.

Brind loped easily along, while the dogs pattered in front, zigzagging the forest floor, noses constantly to the ground. The dog boy was secretly glad to be pulling the litter. Aurélie was no weight, and he could move faster this way than if she were walking alongside him, even if she were fully fit. As he ran, the thrill of relief that Aurélie had survived the plague passed through him again. He was still confused, and hardly dared believe that it was so, but he threw back his head and laughed at the tree tops.

'Plague healer! Plague healer!'

*

The bells of Horsham were audible long before its people came into sight. Church bells, ringing the alarm, even though alarm had already become certainty.

Sir Edmund reined in his horse and herded the hounds off the track, so that the first desperate huddle of townsfolk could trundle past with their handcarts. Others followed, a thin straggle at first, then a whole convoy of hastily loaded wagons and carts, surrounded by distraught faces and crying children: a civilian army in panicked retreat from an enemy that had shocked them with its savagery when they had thought themselves safe. Sir Edmund watched in grim silence, and most of those passing kept their heads down, intent only on their own survival, but a man with a bemused infant on his shoulders and a small boy beside him turned to Sir Edmund as he passed.

'Stay away if you want to live!' he shouted.

'Plague?' asked Sir Edmund, because he felt he should say something.

The man laughed bitterly. 'No, no, not plague. We were saved from the plague by a Black Friar.'

The small boy didn't understand his father's irony and looked up seriously at Sir Edmund.

'Yes, my lord, it is the plague.'

His father strode onwards, pulling the boy with him, and Sir Edmund turned to Lifford.

'So much for murder,' he said coldly.

'It was the friar drowned the Devil's boy, not me,' protested Lifford quickly.

He was watching Sir Edmund's hand, which was resting on his sword hilt. But Sir Edmund didn't draw the sword.

'Devil's boy,' he muttered scathingly, and drove his hounds into the trees, away from the benighted town.

At first, Aurélie thought they had stumbled on a remote castle, but there was no sign of fortifications, no ditch or rampart; and though high, the wall rising through the dusk-darkened trees was not formidable. Craning round in her seat on the litter, she could make out cross-shaped windows and then a bell tower. Aurélie became excited.

'Brind, I think it's a monastery. Or a priory. You know, monks. Nuns.'

Brind had already slowed down warily; now he stopped. He had an idea that monks and friars were the same thing.

'Holy man?' he asked apprehensively.

'He won't be here,' said Aurélie, as if the notion were ridiculous.

After a day of feebleness, she was feeling assertive. She rolled from the litter and stood up. The ground swayed beneath her feet, but finally stopped where it was meant to be. A great arched door was set into the wall near the bell tower and Aurélie looked eagerly towards it.

'Shelter, Brind,' she said encouragingly. 'And food.'

The dogs wagged their tails at their favourite word. And, in truth, Brind had been concerned about finding a place to sleep: Aurélie was too weak to risk another night in the open. But still he hung back, the gathering dark sapping his confidence in his new role as plague healer and making him reluctant to come within harmful reach of further human beings. Even if Brother Rohan would not be one of them. The hounds had been distracted by Aurélie's mention of food, but the dog boy remained watchful, uneasy. Aurélie, however, had made up her mind.

'And they'll know exactly how far it is to Garwood,' she said.

As she walked unsteadily away, Brind left the litter and followed. It somehow seemed wrong to use physical force to stop her.

A knotted rope hung beside the great door and Aurélie hauled on it. She was rewarded by the clanging of a bell somewhere on the other side and almost instantly the door swung open.

Aurélie hesitated for a moment, as the unpleasant thought occurred to her that Brind might be right. What if Brother Rohan *was* here, merely as a traveller, like themselves? But it was unlikely: the place was hidden away miles from the track that the friar had been following. Aurélie beckoned Brind and stepped through the doorway. The dogs also hesitated now, waiting for Brind to join them, before filing after her. Brind leashed Gabion as they went.

It seemed that they had stepped into night. The surrounding walls cut out the last of the twilight and the sky above was black as a closed lid. As their eyes became accustomed to the darkness, Aurélie could make out that they were in a courtyard, cloistered on three sides. Brind saw only shadows. He clutched Aurélie's hand, wanting to drag her back out into the forest, but she tugged him forward.

They were halfway across the courtyard when they heard the great door slam shut behind them and the darkness became sudden, garish light, as flaming torches emerged from every corner. Torches carried not by concerned, hospitable monks, but a circle of unkempt, unsmiling soldiers. At least, Brind and Aurélie took them for soldiers: some of them wore leather hauberks, others chain mail, and all were armed with a variety of weapons.

The circle closed unhurriedly and without a word, until it was little more than a sword's length from the boy and girl and their dogs. Glaive growled threateningly, but Brind's hand stayed him from springing forward.

Then the shaft of a hunting spear was suddenly poked hard in the dog boy's ribs, almost toppling him over. Then another and another. Brind was bewildered. Soldiers began pulling his ears, grabbing at his shabby tunic, contorting their faces grotesquely in what they imagined to be a copy of his own. Still he clung on to the dogs, even though the soldiers tormented them too, prodding them with their spears and laughing uproariously as Gabion inexplicably began chasing his own tail, frantically round and round, until he upended himself and pulled Brind over with him, the belt leash twisted halfway up the dog boy's arm.

'Gentlemen!'

The soldiers instantly stopped their game, the jeers and laughter dying away. The circle parted in front of Brind and Aurélie, and through the gap walked a red-haired woman. Brind struggled to his feet and Aurélie, who had also been subjected to the prodding and teasing, stopped flailing at her tormentors and simply stared. Her eyes were fixed on the imperious new arrival, who wore the boots, breeches and padded jerkin of a warrior. A wide sash of emerald-green silk marked her out as special and complemented the red hair that cascaded around her shoulders and shone like fire in the torchlight.

'Welcome,' she said into the sudden silence, and smiled generously.

There was an explosion of hilarity around the circle, but as the woman stepped towards the children and their dogs, the men fell silent again. She stooped, crouching in front of Glaive, her face a breath away from his jaws, and Aurélie marvelled at her daring.

'My name is Chanterelle,' said the woman, gently scratching the great dog's chin. 'What's yours?'

Glaive bemusedly turned his head and looked up at Brind.

'His name is Glaive,' said Aurélie, trying to copy the woman's calm authority. 'The other dog is Gabion, his son. And this is Brind. And I am Aurélie.'

She had saved herself till last but thought her own name sounded harsh and plain compared with Chanterelle. Nevertheless, the magnificent woman warmed her with a smile. As she did so, a sentry in the bell tower called, and the great door was swung open again to allow two horsemen to duck in below its arch. They reined in their horses in front of Chanterelle, and Brind instinctively shrank back out of the light as he recognized their faces: the wild-boar hunters. The men were carrying a boar now, strung upside down on a pole between them.

'We'd almost given up on meat for supper,' said Chanterelle.

'Kendrick's aim was as poor as ever,' laughed

the first hunter. 'I had to do all the work myself.'

He hacked the cords from the boar's feet so that it fell heavily to the ground. Two of the soldiers carried it away, but, as the hunter made to dismount, his companion grabbed his arm.

'Goss!' he cried, in sudden alarm. 'It's them!'

He was staring at Brind and Aurélie, and addressed the frowning Chanterelle as he backed his horse away.

'When we passed Horsham three days ago there was talk of a Devil's boy, with hellhounds, and a little French witch: plague bringers!'

Instant pandemonium swept the courtyard, the soldiers falling over each other as they retreated from Brind and Aurélie. Those who had actually touched them stared aghast at their own hands, terrified that signs of the plague would already be visible.

'It can't be them, Kendrick!' Goss's scornful voice boomed out above the din. 'The friar drowned the boy and his dogs, and cured the witch!'

'What do friars know?' snorted Kendrick, backing his horse further away still.

Chanterelle alone had remained calm.

'*Are* you the little French witch?' she asked pleasantly.

'I am French,' replied Aurélie, her head high. 'But I am not a witch. The friar is a fool.'

'And the boy?' asked Chanterelle, studying him.

'Brind is the boy, yes. But he doesn't belong to the Devil.'

'No?' said Kendrick. 'There's plague at the town now.'

This assertion caused even greater terror among the soldiers, and Brind felt the familiar chill of dismay. Swords were being drawn and spears snatched up, to keep the Devil's boy and his dogs and the little witch at a safe distance, and to drive them out.

'Stop!' cried Chanterelle. She drew her own sword and glared around the now dangerously frightened circle, then looked up at Kendrick.

'If you have such a low opinion of friars,' she asked, 'why believe the boy belongs to the Devil?'

'He's returned from the dead, hasn't he?' said Kendrick. 'And he has the Devil's mark. The whole town saw it. On his right shoulder.'

'Left,' corrected Goss. 'They said it was the left.'

'Stick him with your hairpin,' suggested Kendrick bravely. 'See for yourself.'

Chanterelle considered Brind again for several moments, then sheathed her sword abruptly. Aurélie could see a jewelled pin, just above Chanterelle's ear, superfluous in the tumble of red hair. But instead of using the pin, Chanterelle took the astonished dog boy's hand, drawing him, stumbling, towards her, and putting her arm around his shoulder. The soldiers gasped in shock and Chanterelle smiled scornfully at their reaction, then turned to Aurélie.

'Come with me,' she said. 'You look hungry.'

And she led Brind from the stunned courtyard, with Aurélie and the dogs following.

The chamber was luxurious, not at all what Aurélie expected to find in a priory.

'Where are the monks?' she asked.

'They fled the plague,' replied Chanterelle. 'We're protecting the priory from outlaws until they return. Enjoy your supper.'

Dishes of bread and cheese had been brought into the chamber behind them, and bones for the dogs.

'And when you've eaten, sleep,' commanded Chanterelle.

After the door had closed and Brind and Aurélie were alone, they looked at each other uncertainly.

Aurélie shrugged. 'Well,' she said, 'we wanted food and shelter.'

Glaive and Gabion were already attacking the bones.

'And she's not afraid of plague bringers. Her soldiers would have killed us.'

Brind couldn't deny any of this. He dropped on his haunches and sank his teeth into a lump of cheese. But he had lost his appetite.

*

'Cowards,' sneered Chanterelle. 'Fools!' Her fierce gaze took in every subdued face along the refectory table. 'Do you think I would embrace the plague?'

When she had entered the refectory, she had been carrying an earthenware jar. Now she placed it on the table before her, almost reverently.

'*This* keeps me safe,' she said quietly. 'It will keep you safe too, each and every man, if you are brave enough to swallow it.'

She drew her dagger and stabbed it deep inside the jar. When she twisted it out again, the blade brought with it a scoop of something dark and fibrous.

'Eat,' she ordered, and Kendrick flinched as the loaded dagger point was thrust towards him.

'What is it?' he asked untrustingly.

Chanterelle ignored the question.

'Eat.' She held the dagger closer. 'Don't you want to be invincible?'

Kendrick reached up cautiously, but at the last moment Chanterelle laughed and pulled the dagger away, and held it in front of Goss instead.

'Theriac!' she cried. 'Have you never heard of theriac? Where is your classical education?'

With a glance at Kendrick, Goss removed the sticky lump from the dagger point and put it slowly into his mouth. He chewed carefully while the company stared at him, but he seemed to have difficulty swallowing.

'You must have encountered a piece of skin,' said Chanterelle. 'That's good.'

Goss swallowed with an unhappy effort. 'Skin?'

Chanterelle nodded. 'You are eating snake meat. The finest, most expensive snake meat in the world. And the most powerful.'

She was moving along the table now, leaning over and depositing a scoop of the treacle-like stuff in front of each man in turn.

'Made from the flesh of the hamadryad, the deadliest of all serpents. And the cause of the plague.'

Chanterelle paused at the end of the table. She had never met or heard of Brother Rohan, and her belief was different, but the unshakeable conviction was the same.

'The serpent is the giver and taker of life,' she told the hushed company. 'The more dangerous the venom, the greater its power to cure. Like the plague itself, the hamadryad comes from the East. It is the hamadryad that spreads the pestilence and, therefore, only *its* flesh will cure and prevent it. So eat and be protected.'

She ran her finger slowly along the dagger blade, collecting the last gobbets of mashed snake meat, and sucked the finger clean before concluding.

'And be ready to take the Devil's boy to those who are not.'

*

Brind woke from a shallow sleep. Aurélie slumbered on, close by. Only Brind could hear the banging of sword hilts and spears, and the roars of delight echoing from the refectory hall below.

8

Hunting

'Good morning.'

Chanterelle's voice was as warm and sweet as honey. She smiled down at Aurélie, who was still drowsily cocooned in furs and silk cushions.

'You obviously slept well.'

As Aurélie nodded and sat up, Chanterelle knelt beside her, frowning solicitously.

'Have you been ill?'

Aurélie was awake enough to be alarmed. Instinctively, she didn't want to mention the plague, and a glance at Brind, who was crouched unhappily close by, confirmed the instinct.

'No, I'm always pale.'

She hoped the marks on her neck and shoulder had faded enough to look like dirt, even in daylight.

'Actually,' she added, 'I did eat some fungus that didn't agree with me.'

'Well, you clearly need rest,' said Chanterelle, in the kind but dominant tone of a nurse who knows best. 'You must stay right where you are.'

'No,' protested Aurélie, 'we must go.'

Chanterelle smiled blandly and shook her head.

'Not today. Lie back and rest. I'll have some breakfast brought up to you.'

She straightened up and turned to Brind, who was mechanically stroking Glaive's head, his other arm around Gabion.

'Can you ride a horse?' she asked.

Brind gave a brief, wary nod.

'Then you may come hunting with us, while Aurélie recovers from the fungus.'

Brind didn't move. He looked anxiously at Aurélie, who didn't know what to say. Her anxiety to hurry on towards Garwood had already been softened. One more day of rest in this so-comfortable bed would complete her cure and enable her to travel twice as fast. Just one more day.

'Brind's a wonderful hunter,' she said, smiling, and instantly felt that she had in some way betrayed him. The look he gave her said as much, but she told herself not to be silly. Staying in the priory made sense. Just one more day.

'Come along, then,' said Chanterelle brightly, and she strode to the door before turning. 'Bring your dogs, of course.'

Reluctantly, Brind stood up and, with another

unhappy look at Aurélie, sloped out of the chamber, Glaive and Gabion at his heel.

'Go down to the courtyard,' said Chanterelle. 'The men will give you some breakfast and find you a horse.'

When Brind had gone, Chanterelle turned back into the chamber. She picked up something that was lying on a chest beside the door and held it up in front of her. It was a dress, finely made of green velvet. The colour was almost the same as the sash that Chanterelle wore across her shoulder.

'I thought you might like this,' she said, and laughed. 'The dress you have on does perhaps need changing.'

Aurélie was thrilled. She took the dress, savouring its lavender-scented smoothness. It was not cloth of gold, but she had never longed to be a fine, fashionable lady. There had been times, though, in the mud and tearing brambles of the forest, when she had longed to be a clean, well-dressed one, and this was the perfect answer.

'Thank you,' she said. Chanterelle had risen even higher in her estimation. 'May I ask you a question?' Aurélie was eager to talk, woman to woman.

Chanterelle nodded graciously and smiled.

'How is it you come to be leading a band of soldiers?'

Chanterelle shrugged. 'My father was killed at Crécy.'

'Mine too!' gasped Aurélie.

'I had no husband, no brothers, mother. I was alone.'

'Me also!'

Aurélie listened intently as Chanterelle sat companionably beside her and continued.

'The men here have all fought in the wars. Some with my father, some not. All have been given promises, not one has been paid. King Edward has no money.' She shared the sarcasm of this last remark with Aurélie, who glowed and nodded in a wordly-wise way. 'The richest landowner in England, in whose name these men were called to fight and die, has no money to pay them. Worse, he has seized my father's land to pay his debts, and so left me homeless.'

Aurélie was outraged. 'In France it would be different!' she cried.

'Then you will understand my anger, my determination to take my father's sword and join with other cheated warriors. To fight for honour and survival.'

'Yes!' exclaimed Aurélie. 'I would fight too!'

Already she could feel the sword in her hand, the green sash across her shoulder, and she endured a pang of irritation when she remembered that she was already engaged on an urgent quest: she had a duty to Sir Edmund that prevented her becoming a warrior here and now.

'And you?' asked Chanterelle. 'Why are you wandering in the forest?' She smiled encouragingly at the eager face beside her. 'Where is it you must go, Aurélie?'

In the courtyard, Brind was greeted with a warmth that utterly bewildered him. Men who the night before had retreated at spear's length now competed to get closest to him, making great show of shaking his hand and putting an arm around his shoulder. Some even patted the dogs.

Food and water were generously provided, and a choice of horse, and although Brind was not entirely trusting of the sudden friendliness, he began to relax a little. At the very least, it was right to let Aurélie rest. And the prospect of charging through the forest, with Glaive and Gabion bounding ahead of Chanterelle's men, lifted his heart. He was proud of his hounds.

'Only the black one.'

Chanterelle's voice behind him was brisk, less kindly than in the bedchamber.

Brind turned to see her approaching. She pointed at Glaive.

'We don't need him as well. But I'd like to use his collar.'

Before Brind could speak, Chanterelle indicated

a door next to the small stable that was built against the courtyard wall.

'Put him in the feed room. Quickly now! And don't forget the collar.'

Brind opened the feed-room door and found brief comfort in the familiar warm smell of hay and bran, as he slipped the collar from the great dog's neck.

'Stay,' he said, pointing, and Glaive slunk inside.

Chanterelle shut the door firmly on the mastiff's questioning look and turned away, climbing nimbly into the saddle of a fine grey horse.

'Mount up, mount up,' she chivvied Brind. 'The day's almost over.'

A dozen or so of her men were already on their horses. They seemed to Brind to be far too heavily armed for hunting boar or deer. Swords and shields were an encumbrance in the forest. But he did as he was told and was at Chanterelle's side as she led her company out through the great arched door, with Gabion running eagerly ahead.

Aurélie could hear the horses clattering away as she lay curled up with her new dress and then drifted into a satisfying dream of the haughty, wealthy Lady Alice, speechless as she welcomed Aurélie to Garwood Manor with her brilliant companion-in-arms, Chanterelle.

*

Several times now both Brind and Gabion had caught the scent of wild boar. Gabion had raced off through the undergrowth, but on each occasion Brind had been required to call him back.

'Gabion find boar,' said Brind.

But Chanterelle merely smiled and shook her head, and kept riding.

'I should like something else today,' she said.

Only when they emerged from the forest at the top of a low hill did she call a halt. Brind looked at her enquiringly. A flat-bottomed valley spread before them, without trees or cover of any kind. As hunting country, it looked most unpromising.

Then Brind noticed the manor house, nestled under the northern slope, the forest around it cleared and in the process of being cleared further, except for a huge oak tree. Brind judged the place to be of similar size to Dowe Manor, though more prosperous-looking. There were sheep in a pen beyond the cow byre, and their melancholy bleating floated across the valley on the still air. For a short while there was no other sound, except the buzzing of flies and the snorting of the horses tormented by them.

Gabion was panting and looked up at Brind. The young dog was thirsty and there was a stream in the valley. Brind was about to ask if they could go to it and drink when Chanterelle spurred forward, leading the company down into the valley at a canter. But she didn't stop at the stream, just splashed straight through it and on towards the homestead.

As they got closer, Brind realized there were children playing in the oak tree. He could hear their laughter and then their cries of fright. The children dropped from the dense foliage like giant fruit and scampered towards the house, two of them hurrying back for the smallest, who had landed heavily and was wailing in panic. The yard gate was open, but Chanterelle didn't follow the children as they tumbled in at the house door. Instead, she reined in outside the yard, holding up her hand to halt the company crowding behind her.

Dogs were barking and two finally put in an appearance, but clearly they were more used to browbeating sheep than seeing off intruders, and they kept well clear of the horses' hooves, and of Gabion, who was getting excited and was not afraid of mongrels.

Chanterelle snatched Glaive's collar from Brind and handed it to Kendrick.

'Get off your horse,' she ordered, and the dog boy obeyed. His stomach churned. He didn't know what was going to happen, why they had come to this place, but he was afraid. Chanterelle again spoke sharply, but not to Brind.

'Kendrick. Are you ready?'

Kendrick nodded, with an unpleasant smile, and

dismounted. When Brind turned back to Chanterelle, she was riding unhurriedly into the yard, alone. Then Kendrick's hand closed on the dog boy's shoulder.

'Stand still, Devil's boy.'

For a bewildered instant, Brind saw Glaive's collar as it passed down over his eyes. Then it was being fastened round his neck.

'No!' he cried, shaking his head violently, trying to break free.

But Goss was holding his arms now, and Brind could do nothing to prevent Kendrick tightening the collar and attaching a leash.

'Heel, boy,' said Kendrick, laughing. 'Heel.'

The man at the manor-house door regarded Chanterelle, but didn't ask her business.

'Is your master at home?' she enquired.

'I am the master.'

He opened the door fully and stepped on to the threshold. The children behind him disappeared quickly into the dark interior of the house. A woman was looking down from a small upstairs window, and two labourers were watching, motionless, at the granary door above the nearby barn. The mongrels had run off.

'I see no black flag flying,' said Chanterelle, glancing around. 'So your household has not been visited by the plague?'

'By God's mercy,' said the man.

His voice was calm, but though he didn't take his eyes off the emerald-sashed warrior woman before him, his hand closed around the hilt of a rusty broadsword propped inside the doorway.

'You will not need that,' Chanterelle assured him pleasantly. 'We mean you no harm.'

The man kept hold of the sword.

'It gladdens my heart that the Devil has not yet touched this place,' continued Chanterelle. 'For it is in my power to keep his evil from you.' She paused. 'Or not.'

The children's faces had appeared with their mother's at the upstairs window. They were in the apple store. Even outside the yard gate, Brind could smell the fermenting remains of last year's fruit. He could also hear the menace in Chanterelle's calm, clear voice.

'Perhaps,' she said, 'news has reached you of the Devil's boy and his hellhound, who killed their master's wife and many other innocents, then brought the plague to Horsham?'

Now Brind finally understood and was appalled. He opened his mouth to howl a protest, but Goss clamped an ungentle hand across his face, muffling the cry.

'Sshh!' Kendrick tightened his hold on the leash, half throttling the distraught dog boy. 'And make sure the hellhound behaves too, or I'll cut his tongue out.'

The man at the door had heard of the Devil's boy. He nodded slowly at the warrior woman, still waiting for the attack that didn't come. 'He drowned,' he said.

Chanterelle shook her head. 'He lives. Hell's fire is not so easily put out.' She smiled. '*This* is the plague bringer!'

And Brind was dragged, struggling and howling, into the yard.

'No! Not plague bringer! Not plague bringer! Plague healer . . .'

But his words were choked in his throat by the roughly tightened collar and the man at the door heard only the guttural growls and howls of a raving creature. He tried to remain calm, sceptical, but he felt his sword hand begin to sweat.

'Touch him, if you doubt me,' invited Chanterelle, as Brind was brought to a halt beside her horse. 'Find the Devil's mark on his shoulder.'

The rest of the grinning company were filling the yard behind her and, rather than appear a coward, the man stepped from his doorway, sword in hand. A panicked shout of protest from his wife at the upstairs window halted him, but Chanterelle propelled Brind towards the man with her foot.

'Touch him,' she jeered.

Brind stumbled forward and for a moment man and boy were staring into each other's frightened eyes. Then Brind whipped around. He lowered his head and ran straight at Chanterelle's horse. He had no plan, no method in his attack, only an overwhelming desire to fight back, to spare the victim and his family. But as his head made contact with the horse's flank, and the excited Gabion leapt and barked beside him, Brind was dragged to the ground by the combined weight of Goss and Kendrick. The latter's voice in his ear was more threatening than ever.

'Play your part, if you want the French girl to live!' Then he pulled the ear savagely, so that Brind had no choice but to look up at him. 'Understand?'

Brind understood, and made no further move to escape, only lay writhing in the dirt, uttering howls of anguish so tormented that even Chanterelle was momentarily chilled.

'Is that not the voice of the Devil?' she cried.

As Brind was hauled to his feet again, the man recoiled and, up above, his wife's screaming became a sobbing entreaty.

'Give them what they ask, husband. Give them what they ask!'

The man leaned against the doorpost, breathing hard. His eyes were on Chanterelle again, avoiding the loathsome, straining, moaning Devil's boy. He refused to grovel, but he had seen children dying of the plague.

'Well?' he said.

Chanterelle smiled. 'I seek no reward,' she said courteously. 'To have kept the plague from this happy household is –'

'Take what you will!' shouted the man, and he stood aside in surrender.

Chanterelle shrugged, then smiled at the strained, shocked faces at the upstairs window.

'It would be ungracious to decline such a generous offer,' she said, and beckoned her men forward.

The company teemed eagerly into the house and barn, and byre and stables, taking everything that wasn't nailed down, and many things that were. They trampled in and out past the now-ignored Devil's boy as he lay curled in misery, while his hellhound dug holes in the beaten earth beside him. And when they had removed every last jewel, gold coin and platter, every chicken, horse and sheep, they pulled the boy upright and dragged him away.

Aurélie could hear a lot of noise. The hunting party had returned. Roast boar for supper, perhaps, or venison. Remembering to lift the hem of her new velvet dress, she hurried happily downstairs. Then came to an astonished halt. No boar, no deer. Instead, the courtyard looked like a marketplace. Chickens clucked, horses were picketed outside the chapel, and she could see sheep penned inside it. Furniture and furnishings were piled everywhere.

The noisy, excited soldiers all had their backs to Aurélie. They were facing a small wagon on which Chanterelle was standing, hair flying, eyes gleaming, flushed with victory. From the pile beside her, she flung items of jewellery and coin to the company, each man nimbly catching his share and jealously watching his neighbour.

'Chanterelle?'

The soldiers fell silent and Chanterelle paused in her distribution of the booty to look across at Aurélie.

'I thought you were going hunting?'

Aurélie's words were met with a roar of laughter and all eyes turned to the mystified French girl.

'So we did,' said Chanterelle. 'Here, this is for you.' She held out a small ruby on a gold chain. 'A girl of about your age gave it to me. Wasn't that kind?' She dangled the jewel. 'Here, take it.'

Aurélie didn't move. The peculiar marketplace was beginning to make a dreadful kind of sense.

'Where's Brind?' Panic was rising inside her.

'He's where he belongs,' said Chanterelle, unconcerned. 'With his dogs.'

More laughter.

'I want to see him.'

'You don't want my gift, then?'

Aurélie shook her head. 'Let me see Brind. I demand to see him.'

The men oohed expectantly. No one spoke to their leader like that.

Chanterelle's voice became dangerously cold. 'Demand?' Then she shrugged and made a mock curtsy. 'As you wish, my lady. Kendrick!'

Aurélie squealed as her arm was twisted painfully up her back. Her kicking feet barely touched the ground as Kendrick marched her across the courtyard. With his free hand he lifted the latch of the feed-room door and flung Aurélie into the musty darkness, where she cracked her head against a wall, then collapsed on a squirming pile of alarmed dogs.

'Brind! Brind, are you here?' she wailed. 'What have they done to you!'

Her groping hands found the dog boy's head. And then the collar around his neck.

It hadn't been easy for Brind to explain, because he didn't have the words. It was even less easy for Aurélie to listen, because she had all too many. Every one of them self-punishing. How could she have been so stupid, so wrapped up in herself and her smiling warrior goddess? She hated herself and felt more deeply ashamed than she had ever felt in her short life. She had been duped, Brind had been used in the most despicable, terrifying way, and now they were both trapped in a windowless prison inside a priory that had been turned into a fortress. There was no escape. Aurélie wished that Brind would shout at her, even set the dogs on her. She wanted to suffer. Instead, out of a long silence, the dog boy growled a single word.

'Dig.'

'What?'

'Dig.' Brind ran his hand across the rough stone beside him. 'Priory wall,' he said softly. 'Dig burrow.'

They waited until the thin line of daylight beneath the feed-room door had faded. Thankfully, nobody came to separate or even feed them. At nightfall, the sentry outside the door gave way to a grumbling replacement. Aurélie recognized Kendrick's voice and hoped fervently he would be blamed when the door was opened in the morning and the prisoners were found to have spectacularly vanished. But she said nothing, just kept out of the way while Brind murmured in Glaive's ear, patted the mastiff's rump and set the great feet, with their nails like sharpened steel, to dig.

The floor of the tiny feed room was compacted, but beneath it the earth was softer. Glaive worked steadily, seeming to understand the need for stealth, but Gabion soon became desperate to take his place, repeatedly scrabbling at the edge of the growing hole, despite Brind's discouraging taps on his muzzle. At last, Brind hauled Glaive backwards and out, and Gabion dived into the hole like a terrier, uttering a pent-up snarl at the quarry he fondly imagined to be deep below. As Gabion disappeared, Aurélie heard the door latch being lifted.

Brind instantly flattened himself across the hole, with Gabion inside. He could feel the dog's tail whipping against his stomach and hoped Gabion wouldn't suffocate. Beside him, Aurélie lay quite still, feigning sleep, an arm around Glaive's taut neck. Beneath him, Gabion was becoming agitated, backing hard against Brind's weight, as the feed-room door swung open.

Kendrick held a flaring torch inside the doorway, illuminating the cobwebbed walls and the bodies of the dogs and children wedged on the floor. He counted the children but not the dogs. The Devil's boy was twitching violently in his sleep. Kendrick crossed himself and wondered how long the theriac worked for. He would make certain he got some more from Chanterelle in the morning. He prodded Aurélie with his foot, and she responded with her best impression of a disturbed snore, and continued to snore in an effort to drown out the strangled sneezes and grunts that she could hear emanating from beneath Brind. To her dismay, Kendrick helped himself to one of the apples that Chanterelle kept in the feed room for her horse. He took a large bite, but as Aurélie silently begged Gabion not to erupt from the floor in front of him, he spat it out again and threw the evidently rotten fruit against the wall with a curse before departing and slamming the door shut behind him.

As the latch dropped into place, Brind rolled aside in the renewed darkness, and Aurélie immediately enveloped Gabion in a calming hug as he shot backwards from the hole. Loud barking would undoubtedly cause Kendrick to return, but Gabion was too sorry for himself to bark, and had certainly had enough of being a terrier, so Glaive was put to digging again, urgently.

Soon, the entrance to the hole had become just large enough for Brind to squeeze in after Glaive. The dog boy did so, blindly tearing out flints and tree roots from the tunnel walls ahead of him, so that he could shift himself further, bit by bit, beneath the priory wall towards freedom.

The foundations were shallow but the wall was thick and Brind was close to exhaustion when, quite suddenly, Glaive's hind feet scrabbled upwards and Brind found himself breathing fresh night air instead of the choking earth. He stretched up his hand, but although he could hear Glaive shaking himself somewhere above, he was unable to stop the great dog from snuffling and sneezing away the soil clogging his nostrils. The noise soon stopped, and Brind felt Glaive's mouth on his hand, as if the dog were trying to pull the rest of the boy from the hole.

Brind clawed and pushed and finally emerged. His tunic was full of soil, and earthworms fell from his hair and ears. Glaive snapped at the worms as Brind grabbed Aurélie's hand as it too emerged from the mound of earth at the base of the wall, a pale mole waving above a giant molehill. For several desperate seconds Aurélie was stuck fast in the tunnel as Brind tried to haul her out: the loathsome velvet dress had snagged on a tree root. Aurélie tore herself free with an effort born of hatred of the woman who had given the dress to her, leaving a sleeve in the tunnel. But as she scrambled to her feet, she heard a high-pitched sigh and then a clatter, and saw that an arrow had narrowly missed her and hit the wall.

Gabion appeared from the tunnel with the sleeve in his mouth. He dropped it at Aurélie's feet, pleased with himself and puzzled at being ignored as another arrow hit the wall, then another, accompanied by loud orders to halt. Then the foliage all around began to shake as sentries clambered quickly down from the tree tops. Their shouts were answered from within the priory wall and the bell began to ring out the alarm. There was no point in remaining silent now; only in running.

The new dress was even more of an encumbrance as Aurélie fled into the forest behind Brind, who had to drag her along, dodging obstacles as he ran. It was dark, but not dark enough. Away from the light of the sentries' torches they might stand a chance of escape, but the sound of hoof beats and harness had already joined the shouting. The entire company had been dispatched to recapture the French girl and the Devil's boy.

Then the moon and the stars suddenly emerged to conspire with the enemy, bathing everything in a ghostly silver light, against which Aurélie and Brind stood out, starkly visible. Moon shadows seemed to dance ahead of them, flickering from tree to tree, before one of them took on more substance and Aurélie, too breathless to shout a warning, tugged at Brind's hand, trying to stop him from running into an ambush.

Brind ran on heedless, assuming Aurélie to be merely tiring, not seeing the shimmering white, man-shaped patch of mist until it stepped out in front of him. If it was a phantom, though, it was a solid one, for its voice was firm and human as it took Brind by the arm.

'This way!' it said urgently, and floated ahead of them, rippling up a slope towards a silver wall.

9

Brother Morice

Solid or otherwise, friend or foe, Aurélie expected the apparition to levitate, to fly across the silver wall, but instead it went straight through it. To her greater astonishment, Brind and the dogs followed. Aurélie charged at the wall with her fists. And rebounded painfully. The surface was cold and hard and smelt of moss. It was not an enchanted silver wall. It was rock. A low cliff.

'Aurélie!'

Brind's voice growled her name and she spun round. All she could see was tier upon tier of hart's tongue fern, growing like a pillar to the top of the cliff. Then Brind appeared from behind the ferns and Aurélie realized that they hid a vertical gash in the rock, little more than a narrow crevice. She eased through after Brind into the dank blackness beyond, and the two of them stood with Glaive and Gabion, listening to Chanterelle's company rampaging through the moonlit forest outside. Only when the sounds of the hunt had faded to nothing did they become aware that the solid white ghost was keeping them company.

'Follow me,' it whispered, and they did so, edging further into the crevice until it became a passage between upright slabs of cold, damp stone, with a narrow floor of hard-trodden earth beneath their feet.

The path sloped downwards and Brind, in front of Aurélie, began to scent the sour fat of a tallow candle. And then something else, faint but unmistakable.

Without warning, the path ended in a small cavern, and there on a broad ledge of rock at the far end, wrapped in a blanket, lay Brother Rohan.

'He cannot harm you.'

The solid white ghost clearly sensed their fear and suspicion. Brind and Aurélie had both stopped dead on recognizing the friar. Glaive growled, and Gabion whined and backed away.

Aurélie looked sharply at the ghost. He was no such thing. Just a pale-faced young man, dressed in a grubby undershirt. His head was shaved in a tonsure. Another friar? Another witch hunter? In league with Brother Rohan, tricking them back into the holy man's clutches?

'Do you know him?'

The question sounded genuine. Aurélie nodded slowly.

'Yes.'

'Then pray for him. He is dying of the plague.'

Aurélie stared at the young man, then turned to Brind. They both looked towards Brother Rohan, only half daring to believe; and only half wanting to.

'My name is Brother Morice,' said the young man, moving away. 'I am a monk. From the priory.'

He shrugged without self-pity as he knelt beside Brother Rohan.

'Now I am a hermit.'

Then he took a handful of moss from the natural basin formed by a hollow in the rock and bathed Brother Rohan's forehead.

The friar didn't move. He was propped against a pile of fresh bracken, and, as their eyes became accustomed to the dim, smoky light in the cavern, Brind and Aurélie saw that the blanket covering him was, in fact, a monk's habit, obviously from Brother Morice's back.

'I found him in the forest yesterday,' continued the young monk. He soaked the moss with water again. 'I think it won't be long.'

'Idiots!' screeched Chanterelle, and her soldiers flinched from the simple word.

The last of them had straggled in from their fruitless search and they stood huddled in the refectory like guilty sheep, while Chanterelle stalked back and forth, kicking over benches in her unbridled anger.

'You have all betrayed me! Every single one. Did I not make you invincible? Did I not share my knowledge? My theriac! I gave you the most potent, the most elegant weapon you have ever had. I gave you riches without bloodshed. And the promise of more. And now there will *be* no more. Because you have thrown it all away as surely as tipping a fortune into the sea!'

She swept a great candle from the table and the men flinched again in the dying light. Every one of them wanted to protest that it was all Kendrick's fault. He was the night sentry guarding the feed room. It was obvious that the prisoners would try to burrow out. At least, it was now. Yes, Kendrick's fault, definitely. And the other sentries, of course. Then again, it had been Chanterelle's decision to shut the Devil's brood in the feed room in the first place. But nobody was going to mention that. Kendrick astonished them all by speaking out.

'We'll find them in daylight,' he said casually.

Chanterelle turned to him and smiled. The candle had revived where it lay at her feet, turning her face into a disembodied mask.

'Will we, Kendrick? How very reassuring.'

Her voice was icy now, but Kendrick was not afraid of Chanterelle, or told himself he wasn't. He and Goss had joined the company only days ago, but he was already irked by the unthinking awe in which the others held their leader. Perhaps the moment had come. She was only a woman, and a mad one at that.

'Besides,' he said, 'I for one am glad they've gone.'

The shocked silence around him only spurred him to say more.

'The trick worked well enough, but it's unmanly. Hiding behind a boy and a dog. We are fighting men, so let us *fight* for what we take.'

'Do you say I am afraid to fight!' Chanterelle's anger flared again, and Kendrick saw the dagger flash from her belt.

'No.'

'I think you do, Kendrick. I think you doubt me as a warrior.' The dagger point was at his throat. 'Well, I will show you how I fight for what I take. Is that what you want?' She turned to the company, shouting, 'Is that what you all want!'

The men didn't know the correct answer, so said nothing.

'Then we leave this vile place at dawn,' cried Chanterelle, as if the answer to her question had been a resounding yes. 'I am as sick of it as I am of you!'

She marched to the door, then turned, pointing the dagger at them all.

'I shall lead you to another pot of gold. But some of you may die before we seize it!'

After the door had slammed behind Chanterelle, Kendrick ventured a knowing smile, as if implying the weakness of hysterical women. But he received only stony looks in return, even from Goss.

Brother Morice had been working on the vegetable plot when Chanterelle's company had attacked the priory two weeks ago. Of the twenty monks who made up the community, half had been killed, including the prior himself. The rest had run away. Only Brother Morice had remained close by, taking refuge in the hidden cavern that in more peaceful times had been used by the monks as a place of solitary meditation.

'I had heard such companies existed in France,' he said, and shrugged. 'Now they are here.'

'Outlaws,' said Aurélie, her voice bitter. 'Criminals. Murderers.'

'We are all sinners,' said Brother Morice mildly.

'Yes,' agreed Aurélie, vehemently missing the philosophical point. 'This holy man tried to kill us both.'

But although Brother Morice nodded sympathetically as Aurélie recounted the friar's many crimes, it made no difference to the gentle care he administered. He had been right, though:

it wasn't long. Before dawn, he straightened up, having bathed Brother Rohan's glistening head for the last time, and looked towards Aurélie and Brind, clearly expecting them to join him at the rough bedside.

Brother Rohan suddenly peered up at the children as they cautiously approached, forcing his glazed, fevered eyes to focus. The faces above him loomed large and ill-defined, as if seen through quivering water, then slid away to become part of the roof of the cavern. There they stuck, small and rebellious, like gargoyles, water dripping from their ugly mouths. And for a moment he remembered everything, or almost everything that mattered to him.

Illness had been a shock. He had come to think himself untouchable. Not immortal, for that would have been blasphemous. But protected by his proven power to hunt down and destroy the Devil's plague bringers. Paradise, so close now, was less attractive than the preaching of it, but if he was to die, Brother Rohan wanted not absolution from his sins, because he admitted none, but confirmation that he had been right. He wanted it desperately, as if it were the key to Heaven, and as his legs kicked involuntarily at the makeshift blanket, he stretched his hand towards the girl. She had floated down from the roof again. No longer a gargoyle but an angel, an angel of his making.

He recognized her clearly now. His uncomfortable misgivings after she had disappeared from him in the forest while he dealt with Lifford now seemed laughable. Brother Rohan struggled for several seconds, his mouth moving painfully before the words were eventually forced out.

'Tell me that I saved you.'

The girl stood in silence. She didn't take his flailing hand. But in the end she replied.

'Yes, Brother Rohan. You saved me.'

He lay back, inwardly rejoicing, although his face could no longer register emotion. But before his eyes lost focus for the final time, another face he recognized appeared beside the girl.

The dog boy from Dowe Manor. The Devil's boy. Alive. With his black hellhound beside him.

Brother Rohan's final breath was a soundless cry of panic.

Sir Edmund wasn't mistaken: it *was* his second best horse, the one he'd given to Brother Rohan, grazing placidly in a clearing with no saddle on its back.

Lifford's vindictive heart leapt and he forgot himself so much as to grab Sir Edmund's arm.

'Allow me, my lord,' he insisted. 'I am lighter on my feet. Keep the hounds still.'

And he slipped from his saddle, ran fleetly across the clearing past the solitary horse and disappeared into the trees. The friar wouldn't get the better of him this time. Lifford clenched the hunting stock in both fists, testing its pliancy and anticipating the pleasure of squeezing the breath from the holy man in revenge. The quarterstaff would have been better, but this would do.

But there was no holy man. The miller searched in stealthy, ever-widening circles without success. He was disappointed and intrigued in equal measure, and completely oblivious to Sir Edmund, left fretting with his hounds and his second-best horse. Then, as he stooped to examine what he thought might be tracks in a patch of mud, Lifford heard a movement behind him. Turning, he could see only a cluster of holly bushes, their dark green leaves glossy and dense. The miller stood up slowly and crept towards the holly. He heard movement again: feet shifting in the leaf mould.

With a shout, he lunged forward, thrashing with the hunting stock. He struck flesh, but the startled cry of pain wasn't human. And, forcing his way between the holly branches, Lifford found himself confronting not a friar but a fretful packhorse, its halter and the ropes of its canvas packs hopelessly entangled among the bushes, the frayed blue ribbon in its mane unravelled by its struggles.

As the trapped, exhausted animal tried vainly to back away from him, the miller began to laugh. He couldn't remember being so happy in his entire life.

Sir Edmund's impatient, demanding voice drifted to Lifford through the trees. The miller quickly tore the entangling holly branches aside and pulled the packhorse away. And by the time the querulous old knight arrived at the holly, Lifford had circled back to his sorrel mare.

Sir Edmund turned sharply, catching the sound of departing hooves. Nonplussed but angry, he retraced his steps as fast as his grinding knees would carry him and, with a shouted command at the dogs, clambered into the saddle.

Lifford heard the hounds behind him, but he was too elated to care. He was, quite suddenly, entirely free; had achieved the true freedom that only wealth could provide. He no longer cared what had happened to the treacherous friar, no longer needed to curry favour with the gruff, stiff-backed old knight. He would ride to London with his canvas packs stuffed with fine furs and cloth of gold. He would become a respected merchant, perhaps. He would certainly live in luxury for the rest of his days.

The forest floor became steep and stony, falling away towards a river, probably the same river in which the dog boy had drowned. Lifford rejoiced: everything was being made easy for him. The river was wide and would snatch his scent away from the hounds, should the old knight seek to pursue him in earnest. He turned downstream to where the rapid sparkling water shouldered its way between sturdy flat-topped boulders. The stone shone wet in the early-morning sun, a glittering causeway leading to the northern bank, to a new life. The miller knew he could cross it. He urged the sorrel mare on to the causeway and pulled the reluctant packhorse after him by its halter.

But although the sorrel mare was nimble, she grew increasingly nervous as the surging river slapped at her hooves. With safety only ten steps away she missed her footing, trapping a hoof in a gap between the boulders and jolting the miller from her back as she lurched sideways. Lifford fell into the river, still clinging to the halter, and so pulling the terrified packhorse after him. The beast was instantly turned on its back by the weight of its canvas-covered burden and sank with its hooves thrashing the air above. Sank on top of Lifford. The racing water was no more than shoulder-deep, but it might as well have been ten fathoms, as Lifford drowned with his legs pinned to the river bed by the spent packhorse and the heavy bales of fur and cloth of gold that were to have been his fortune.

Sir Edmund reined in at the river bank, staring at the statuesque and sunlit sorrel mare that stood in the middle of the river. For a moment he thought it must be some kind of vision, a mythical creature that had appeared in southern England by mistake, because it seemed to be floating on a cloud of gold. Sir Edmund dismounted and, leaving his best and second-best horses tethered, and the hounds lapping at the water's edge, made his way cautiously on to the boulders.

As he approached it, Sir Edmund recognized the floating gold cloud for what it was. He crouched and hauled the unravelling cloth of gold from the river. And as he pulled it clear, he could see what lay beneath it: Lifford and the packhorse, swaying lifeless among the slowly escaping contents of the canvas packs.

'Perhaps the merchant was the plague bringer,' said Aurélie.

She should have been praying. The serious, gentle young monk had just buried Brother Rohan and they were standing at the graveside with heads solemnly bowed. But Aurélie's act of grace towards the dying friar was long forgotten. Having helped drag his body from the cavern, she would have sooner left it to rot than give it proper burial, and her mind had wandered to the cause rather than the fact of his death. She hadn't meant to speak out loud, but continued nonetheless.

'The cloth merchant, Brind. He was at Dowe Manor. He was at Horsham. You said the charcoal burner had met him. And Brother Rohan met him too. Well, his body anyway.' She frowned and shrugged. 'Perhaps the cloth of gold was cursed.' She didn't really believe in curses, but her theory had run out of logic.

Brind didn't answer. He was preoccupied with the uncomfortable thought that he'd made no attempt to heal Brother Rohan as he had healed Aurélie. He told himself that it had been too late, the poison too far spread, which was true; but he couldn't escape the reality that if the dying man had been anyone other than Brother Rohan, he would have tried.

Brother Morice crossed himself and looked at Aurélie with only mild disapproval for her interruption.

'I'm keeping you from your journey,' he said. 'You should have gone by now: patrols come out early from the priory. Do you remember the way?'

Brind and Aurélie both nodded. Brother Morice had given them precise directions. He had passed Garwood Manor once while on pilgrimage to Canterbury.

'Then go with God!'

And he gestured them away.

When the children and dogs had disappeared, Brother Morice wondered briefly if he should have gone with them. But prayer was his vocation, even though the forest was now his chapel. He knelt and prayed for the dead; and for the living.

*

Brother Morice was still praying, with an intensity and abandonment of self that Brother Rohan would have found naïve and ridiculous, when he felt rather than heard approaching horses and, looking round, saw the red-haired warrior woman who had cut down his Father Prior riding unhurriedly towards him. Her entire company was riding at her back, and beyond them he saw a cluster of loaded wagons. Brother Morice stood up and faced his oppressors. He had fled once; he would not flee again.

Chanterelle looked down at the scrawny monk and smiled. She didn't recognize him, but she despised him nonetheless, as she despised all his kind for their meek acceptance of everything. This particular example seemed ready to embrace martyrdom.

'Good morning, Little Brother,' she said. 'I thought you had all run off squealing to the Pope. Those of you who still had legs.'

The men behind her laughed, relieved that last night's fury had given way to cruel humour. They liked cruel humour.

'What kept you here?' asked Chanterelle.

'Prayer,' replied Brother Morice.

Chanterelle cocked her head. 'And what do you pray for, Little Brother?'

'Understanding,' said the young monk, as if the question were a serious one. 'Guidance.'

Chanterelle nodded slowly and smiled again. 'Do you not pray for the return of your beloved priory?'

Brother Morice paused before answering. 'I pray for God's will to be done.'

Chanterelle laughed. 'Well, today *my* will is done.'

She drew her sword and Brother Morice closed his eyes. But no killing thrust followed. Instead, the flat of the sword touched each of his shoulders lightly.

'Arise, *Sir* Little Brother,' commanded Chanterelle. 'The priory is yours. Take it!'

She laughed at his evident confusion, waved her sword behind her and spurred her horse away. Her men followed, bowing to Brother Morice in mock reverence as they passed him, then galloped to overtake their baggage wagons, which had continued lumbering through the forest while Chanterelle made conversation with the monk.

Brother Morice gazed in the direction of the priory. Was it possible? Were the desecrators actually leaving? Then he smelt smoke. He couldn't be sure where it was coming from, so he ran back to the cliff and scrambled up the rocky slope behind it until he stood at the very top of the column of hart's tongue fern. He could see the bell tower now. There were no sentries on it. Only licking tongues of flame.

*

Goss and Kendrick had volunteered to fire the building. It was one way, as Kendrick said, of tidying the place up. The company had made such a mess of it.

They started the blaze in the refectory, where there was plenty of wood, dragging the tables together and placing the prior's chair on top of the heap. Then they had begun other fires in the stable and the cursed feed room, and the chapel, which was the dirtiest of all, having been used as a sheep pen.

The great arched door was standing wide open as Brother Morice arrived, smoke billowing out through it from the courtyard. He shrank back on seeing two horses still tethered by the cloister. The horses were prancing nervously, increasingly alarmed by the smoke and heat. Then two men appeared. They ran to the horses and clambered into their saddles. Riding out, they turned beyond the arch for a final admiring look at their handiwork.

'Well, Kendrick,' said one, 'you have your way. No more plague-bringing. You are a leader in the making.'

'Perhaps,' replied the other. 'If our warrior queen should unfortunately die at Garwood.'

They both laughed and turned their horses away, but, as they did so, they saw a shaven-headed scarecrow, standing against the wall with nowhere to hide. A monk. Kendrick didn't enquire where he had come from; he simply charged at him, and rode him down, and left him lying in the smoke and dust.

Battle

'Find Aurélie!' cried Sir Edmund. 'Find her, you brave brutes!'

He was brandishing Aurélie's scarf as he stood in the middle of the pack, buffeted by the hounds as they jostled each other to get close to the length of red woollen cloth. In the absence of Glaive, Gabion's mother, Ballista, was pack leader, and Sir Edmund made sure she had longest with the scarf at her nose to absorb the scent.

'Find!' he roared, and the diligent manner in which the mastiffs streamed away through the forest behind Ballista gave him hope.

Sir Edmund remounted his best horse and galloped after the disappearing pack with his second-best horse labouring alongside. He'd left the sorrel mare grazing in the forest. He regretted the loss of Lifford, if only because the miller would have been an ally in dealing with Brother Rohan. But Sir Edmund had fought at Crécy, or tried to, and was not deterred by the prospect of single combat with an overweight friar. The smoke in the distance did perturb him, though: the pack seemed to be heading straight towards it.

When Aurélie had first urged the need to go to Garwood, Brind had agreed but not fully understood. Now, having encountered Chanterelle and her men, he truly appreciated the threat of such companies and was convinced that Chanterelle herself would somehow find her way to Dowe Manor. He could picture the helpless terror on poor Milda's face as the ruthless soldiers swept down on her. And Sir Edmund's brave but futile resistance. They had to be protected, reinforced as quickly as possible. Brind broke into a run, then checked himself as Aurélie called wearily behind him. She stretched out her hand and he took it, pulling her along.

Brind wished they still had the litter. Aurélie wished she had said less to Chanterelle. Brind mistook her miserable expression for fatigue and shared anxiety about their home. But Aurélie had another, deeper worry that she hadn't yet shared with the dog boy. She hoped she wouldn't have to.

Chanterelle thought her father would have been proud of her. Everything she had told Aurélie about him was a pack of lies. He would have been proud of that too. He'd been a man-at-arms who deserted King Edward's army long before Crécy, forming a gang with like-minded fellow-soldiers, and attacking and robbing French civilians where and when he chose. The pickings had been even richer back in England, and Chanterelle, his only surviving child, bold and grasping since birth, had demanded a place at his side. When her father had died, with his head in a puddle of wine rather than in combat, his men had accepted Chanterelle as leader, seeing in her the same savage intelligence and lack of scruple.

Now she was commanding a veritable army, because since leaving the priory the company's ranks had been swollen by two other, smaller bands, who'd been impressed by the baggage train and the fresh meat still on the hoof. Chanterelle was on campaign and the next battle was to be fought on ground of her choosing. The emerald-green banner flying above her head thrilled her with its perverted nobility. She wondered if the little French witch, who had stolen a dress from her, had been foolish enough to continue her own journey to Garwood. How satisfying if she had.

Sir Edmund had first glimpsed the bell tower some minutes ago. Now it came into view again, briefly, before collapsing. The noise rumbled lazily towards Sir Edmund through the forest, but though he listened intently above the calling of the hounds, he could hear no shouts or cries, human or animal, no reaction at all to the collapse. He dreaded what he would find if Aurélie were there. The pack still seemed certain enough, closing in on the apparent disaster, and Sir Edmund followed.

Soon the priory wall appeared and Sir Edmund could hear the fire inside it; not a raging noise now, just a comfortable hiss and crackle, as if the priory were a giant hearth. The fire was dying, its work done.

The hounds had come to a halt, barking frustratedly, the scent masked by the fire, the ground scorched hot beneath their feet. Sir Edmund dismounted. The priory wall was warm to the touch as he edged around it towards the great arched doorway, where the door itself had perished and its two posts had been reduced to blackened stumps.

Sir Edmund stopped. Something was lying in the dust outside the doorway. For a moment he thought it was a heap of brown sacking. Then he saw the feet.

Brother Morice was extremely thirsty. He had thought himself halfway to Heaven, or perhaps that had been a dream. Certainly, the thumping headache was earthly enough, as if he'd been kicked by a horse. He remembered what had happened and tried to move. But his chest had been kicked as well, and a broken rib jagged inwards sharply, causing him to wince. Then, miraculously, a pigskin full of water was pressed to his mouth. Brother Morice drank until he choked, which caused the rib to stab him again. He examined his Good Samaritan cautiously: an elderly man with a broad, lined face and grey hair. Dressed like a soldier, a sword laid on the ground beside him. He had a pack of dangerous-looking dogs as well, but he seemed to come in peace, though his voice was gruff and urgent.

'Have you seen a young girl here?'

Brother Morice hesitated.

'Speak, damn you!'

Sir Edmund was in no mood for the niceties of respectful address, particularly with those who wore habits, black or otherwise.

'Who are you, my lord?'

'I'm her guardian!' roared Sir Edmund. 'Now speak, or I'll set the dogs on you!'

Brother Morice sensed desperation rather than vicious intent. He made up his mind and answered, even though the Good Samaritan didn't fit Aurélie's description of her guardian as frail and helpless.

'She has gone to Garwood Manor.'

The Good Samaritan fell back on his heels. He appeared both shocked and confused.

'The friar has taken her to Garwood?'

'The friar is dead. She has gone with the boy and his dogs.'

The Good Samaritan peered at Brother Morice, his frown and confusion deepening.

'You are delirious, Brother. It's the boy who is dead.'

Brother Morice shook his head emphatically, braving the pain. 'Brind is alive.'

The Good Samaritan looked away.

'Garwood,' he muttered, as if unable to digest more than one shock at a time. He creaked to his feet and turned away. 'Garwood . . .'

Brother Morice quickly plucked at his arm.

'My lord, the woman who did this is also riding to Garwood.'

The Good Samaritan looked from the monk to the devastated priory and back again.

'Woman?' It was one shock too many.

Garwood Manor glowed. It glowed in the most glorious sunshine. But the warm beauty of such an evening annoyed rather than delighted Lady Alice Garwood, because it spoilt her claim that the weather, like the world itself, had gone entirely to the bad. Everything had been better when she was young, the only exception to this rule being that when she was young she had been married to the tiresome Sir John Garwood and now she was a widow: arrogant, selfish and with the tightest purse strings in southern England, if not the entire civilized world. And because she spent nothing, Lady Alice had accumulated a fortune. When she was young, the estate had been worked by unpaid serfs. But labour had become scarce because of the wars, and now the confounded plague, and ignorant labourers had developed the effrontery to demand wages. That was another thing: there had been no plague when Lady Alice was young. So she made do without labour now, selling her outlying farms and keeping her money within the four walls of her manor house, where it could be counted, daily.

Aurélie knew that Lady Alice was rich. She had fondly imagined that consequently there would be loyal men-at-arms at Garwood, or, at the very least, sturdy yeoman, who could be dispatched to the rescue of defenceless Dowe Manor. But there was only a decrepit gardener and his equally decrepit wife. And a thin-lipped old lady with jewels in her tightly coiled hair, squinting into the annoying golden sun.

Because of the sun, Lady Alice could not see the two children and two dogs emerging from the forest at the western end of the valley. Because of the forest itself, she could not see Chanterelle's scouts gazing down from the northern ridge. And because she had not seen or thought of him in thirty years, she could not have imagined Sir Edmund Dowe galloping towards her with a bandaged monk as his squire. She turned her back on the sun and went to find the gardener, thinking of something to complain about as she went.

Brind and Aurélie paused on seeing Garwood for the first time. The end of their journey. Strength and comfort. Success. It sat secure in its sunlit valley, as if existing in a different world entirely from the mud and rain and terror outside it. Chanterelle was not there. The guilty fear that she had told Chanterelle too much about Garwood shrivelled in Aurélie's mind, so that she smiled at Brind in relief. He smiled back, and Aurélie found the strength to run from the trees towards the distant house, and Glaive and Gabion ran too, sensing a sudden, unfamiliar burst of happiness and barking as a means of sharing in it.

Ballista heard the barking and so did Sir Edmund. In the hope of outflanking the warrior woman and her army, the old knight had circled further south and was now climbing the ridge on the southern side of the valley. Brother Morice did his best to follow. He wasn't used to horse-riding and his head didn't like the jolting. He wasn't sure why he had joined Sir Edmund: he couldn't imagine fighting. But he had to admit that the red woollen scarf, bound tightly around his chest by the old knight to support the injured rib, gave him a rather dashing appearance. For a monk, at least.

Of all the startling information that Brother Morice had given Sir Edmund, the most astonishing was that Aurélie perceived Garwood as a source of help. But that was his fault, because he had never told her otherwise. It hadn't occurred to him, just as it hadn't occurred to him to inform Lady Alice of his wife's death. Alice had shown no interest in her younger sister when alive; and her stated belief of thirty years ago that Beatrice had married beneath herself still rankled. And, absurdly petty though it was, the first thing that came into Sir Edmund's mind as he rode from the trees on the ridge top and looked down on the smug, well-proportioned Garwood, a manor more like a palace, was that his sister-in-law, on her one and only visit to Dowe, had described *his* home as more like a farmhouse.

Then, looking to his left, Sir Edmund saw the children in the valley below. And, above them, a dark ripple along the tree line. At first, he thought the ripple was just the lengthening shadow of the forest on the opposite ridge, but then he saw the banner and realized that he and Brother Morice were outnumbered fiftyfold. Even at Crécy, the odds had been only five to one.

*

Things could not have worked out better for Chanterelle. The children were still a long way from the manor house, totally exposed. She would deal with them first, then attack the manor. If there was resistance there, so much the better: she had promised her soldiers bloodshed, as well as gold.

'Kill!' she cried, and, with an answering shout, her army poured after her down the slope towards their quarry, out of the shadows and into glorious, killing light.

'Brind!' Sir Edmund's agonized roar was lost in the clamour of horses and men cascading from the opposite ridge.

On the valley floor, Brind and Aurélie halted, shocked by the sudden eruption of Chanterelle's army above them and its sheer size.

The wave of cavalry rolled down towards them, dividing itself into three equal parts with the evident intention of surrounding its helpless prey. And although Glaive was immediately ready for the fight, snapping and snarling as he backed protectively against Brind, he was one against many. Gabion was bewildered and followed Aurélie and Brind as they raced towards the southern slope, the only part of the valley not yet cut off to them.

'I'm sorry!' sobbed Aurélie, as they ran. But Brind didn't understand what she meant.

Suddenly, Gabion found a purpose other than retreat, barking at Brind and Aurélie as he bounded ahead and back again, as if calling them on. And looking beyond the excited dog to the brow of the hill, Brind saw not only Sir Edmund and a red-sashed Brother Morice, but the finest pack of mastiffs in all of England.

Behind Brind, Aurélie had fallen. The velvet dress had tripped her, and for a bitter moment she thought it no more than she deserved, but then Gabion raced back loyally to her and as he did so, Brind stopped climbing the hill and howled. It was not a sound of pain or despair now, but a rallying call, and every hound responded, almost unseating Sir Edmund as they surged past him, a yapping, volatile rabble instantly transformed into a deadly phalanx of muscle and teeth.

Sir Edmund could hardly bear to watch. The memory of Crécy, when his hounds had been massacred, had made him hesitate, almost fatally. But Brind had taken charge now. Brind, the loyal servant so unjustly banished. Brind, the dog boy. Brind!

Yelling the name as his battle cry, Sir Edmund raised his sword and charged down the hill behind his hounds.

To the soldiers on the opposite slope, who had been expecting an easy slaughter, Brind now suddenly appeared a frightening prospect. He stood alone, a stark, mysterious figure, made tall by the last slanting rays of the sun. His raised arms cast long black shadows across the hillside, and out of those shadows, as if from cracks in the earth, he summoned the hounds of Hell.

As the men faltered in their charge, the boy pointed across the open ground and the giant hounds left him, loping shoulder to shoulder towards them. Theriac, they believed, had saved them from the plague bringer, but now he sent them death by other means. The dogs made no sound as they ran, which unnerved the soldiers further. Were they real? Or phantoms at the whim of the Devil's boy? Then, twenty paces from them, the dogs gave ominous voice, their feet shook the ground, and the soldiers knew, too late, that they were real enough.

'Kill!' screamed Chanterelle. But it was the dogs that did the killing, not her army.

As horses reared and squealed, and soldiers yelled and hacked at the enraged mastiffs swirling around them, Kendrick tried to get close to Chanterelle. He didn't mind disaster here; in defeat, a leader should die with her troops. He had the knife ready; no one would notice in the heat of battle. The dogs were a fine distraction. When Chanterelle was dead, he would seize the banner and lead a dignified retreat. Once clear away, the company would regroup around him and the future would be his. He was close behind her now, but, as he drew the knife from beneath his cloak, an old knight he vaguely recognized, with an unkempt beard, barged his horse between Chanterelle and her would-be assassin. He swung his sword at Kendrick in a clumsy, avoidable way, but Kendrick was caught with only a knife for defence and the second rustic blow knocked him from his horse. His screams alerted Chanterelle, but when she wheeled her horse there was nothing to be seen except a snarling mound of dogs. Chanterelle ducked the old knight's next swing and spurred her horse away. Those of her army not yet torn from the saddle were already doing likewise. They had a strong pedigree in desertion.

Sir Edmund was disconcerted for a moment by the fact that he'd tried to strike a woman, but there was no resemblance between this creature and his idea of womanhood, so he gave chase and tried to strike again. Disgrace to her kind or otherwise, though, the red-haired woman rode faster than he could and quickly gained the shadowy trees from where she'd first appeared. The old knight saw Aurélie, darting back and forth, alone and vulnerable on the edge of the battlefield, and galloped towards her instead. Let the woman go. He still had his family to protect: he owed them that at the very least. Sir Edmund swiped lustily at the scattered enemy as he went.

Goss had witnessed Kendrick's hideous death and, shrewdly as he thought, was now fleeing against the tide, running up the southern slope, from where the hounds had first attacked. His horse had been taken down, but he himself had been luckier then most, certainly luckier than Kendrick: he was still alive. Cresting the ridge, he saw only trees and safety ahead of him, until the shaven-headed scarecrow, now startlingly draped in red, leapt out in front of him and swung a lump of wood. As he hit the ground, Goss saw Glaive, the biggest hound of all, bounding towards him and knew how it must feel to be an injured rat, trapped on the floor of a barn, when the dogs are let in.

Sir Edmund scooped up Aurélie and seated her in front of his saddle with a dexterity that secretly amazed him. He'd never managed such a feat in his life, despite having practised endlessly as a young man. He turned his horse and scanned the thinning battlefield. Brind was calling off the dogs now, letting the remains of Chanterelle's army scramble on to their surviving horses, two and even three to a mount; and escape. Sir Edmund wouldn't have been so charitable.

'My lord, I can't find Gabion!' Aurélie's voice was tearful. 'Is he dead?'

All the corpses that Sir Edmund could see were human or horseflesh, but there was no sign of a living Gabion. Glaive loped by from the ridge top, responding to Brind's call. His son didn't follow.

Chanterelle watched from the forest fringe as the dog boy joined the old knight and the French girl. She'd had fleeting hopes of Aurélie. Her savage pride would not admit to wistfulness, but Chanterelle felt suddenly empty. And alone. She reminded herself that she still possessed a baggage train stuffed with booty, halted in the forest behind her. There would be opportunity for revenge; she was still free to do whatever she pleased. She dragged her horse round and dug in her heels, whereupon the horse reared violently, prancing backwards on its hind legs, away from something that had sprung in front of it on the track.

The horse plunged forward and Chanterelle, clinging to its neck, came briefly face to face with the black hellhound. Gabion barked once and the horse reared again, throwing Chanterelle from its back in a helpless arc. The horse bolted into the trees as its rider's head hit the ground.

Rain began to patter in the sudden silence. Gabion growled warily and padded forward. The red hair was becoming redder and, when Gabion sniffed at the motionless head, the green cycs didn't blink.

*

Lady Alice was glad of the sudden downpour. It gave her a certainty to cling on to. That and the fact that her brother-in-law had not aged well, as she'd predicted he wouldn't thirty years ago. She'd had no option but to invite Sir Edmund in, and to agree when he insisted that not only the suspicious-looking French girl but the peculiar dog boy too should come into the house. She'd drawn the line at the monk, who was not, by any stretch of the imagination, family. But he seemed to prefer to stay outside on his own, in any case. The hounds were penned in the vegetable garden, where, no doubt, they would cause untold damage.

The frugal supper that the gardener's wife served them was taken in near silence, the victors of the bloody battle now shocked and subdued rather than triumphant, and Lady Alice's heart too deeply encrusted in meanness for her to express more than grudging gratitude for Garwood's deliverance. It suited her better to blame Brind and Aurélie for leading the cut-throats to her idyllic valley in the first place.

Sir Edmund couldn't wait to leave and Lady Alice's protest was minimal when he suggested they should start the journey back to Dowe immediately, in the rain and dark. Then he remembered there were graves to be dug and put back the departure until morning.

'You should spend some money on guarding this

place,' he said gruffly. 'There are plenty of soldiers for hire. Not every man returning from the wars is a villain.'

Lady Alice tutted.

'By the way,' added Sir Edmund, 'your sister's dead.'

He was immediately ashamed of his seeming callousness, but he had always struggled not to descend to Alice's level, and always failed.

'The plague?' She sounded irritated, as if dying of the pestilence was just the sort of thing Beatrice would do.

'Yes.'

Sir Edmund took himself outside into the cooling rain.

In the night, the dogs suddenly started barking, churning up the neat rows of cabbages as they leapt at the wooden fence. Brother Morice was already on his feet with his lump of wood as Sir Edmund and Brind tumbled from the house. But the intruder had no hostile intentions. It was Gabion. And while the young hound and Aurélie enjoyed a lengthy reunion, Sir Edmund led Brind and Brother Morice out into the now moonlit valley and began to dig. By dawn, the valley floor was scarred but empty, and Dowe Manor beckoned more strongly than ever.

Sir Edmund bade his sister-in-law a curt but

polite farewell, repeated his advice on Garwood's safety and climbed on to his horse. Brind and Aurélie had already marshalled the hounds and were leading them away beneath a sky of eggshell blue.

'I've been thinking,' said Lady Alice. Her gimlet eye snapped from Sir Edmund to the thin, gaunt monk beside him. He seemed appropriately austere. 'My sister's soul will need praying for. I don't suppose you've thought to endow a chantry?'

Assuming Sir Edmund's stunned silence to mean that he hadn't, she continued.

'Well, it must be done. And if you won't do it, I shall have to. Someone has to do what's right where family's concerned.'

Sir Edmund said nothing. He was still as sullen as Lady Alice remembered.

'I shall design the chantry myself,' she said. 'And give you some plate to pay for its construction. Make sure you get a good price. Whatever's left may be used to feed the chanter.' She nodded sharply at Brother Morice. 'He'll do.'

Milda scraped the shrivelled remains of marigold and honeycomb into the fire. She would mix some more tomorrow. It had clearly worked, because she hadn't been touched by the plague, but it needed to be fresh.

She'd grown used to being on her own. Sir

Edmund had been troubled about leaving her, but as each day had passed without incident, Milda had relaxed and come to think of herself as mistress of Dowe. She had even taken to talking graciously to herself, as a mistress should talk to a servant.

The sudden clatter of hooves shattered this cosy make-believe and threw Milda into a terrified panic. She peered fearfully out of the kitchen doorway, then squealed in the most ungracious delight as she saw Aurélie and Brind. And if there had been no celebration at Garwood, there was celebration at Dowe. The great hall was reopened, a huge fire lit in its hearth, and, as dusk fell, the damp, draughty room was filled with smoke, warmth and laughter. And enormous helpings of roast venison, for Brind and the hounds had hunted all the way home.

Thrillingly, Milda was commanded to dine with the master rather than in the kitchen; and in Brother Morice she discovered a holy man who restored her faith in holy men, even though he looked far more like Death than Brother Rohan once had.

As he watched the strange human assortment who shared his hall and his life, Sir Edmund worried briefly that Aurélie had been right: Dowe was defenceless. But that had only been so when Sir Edmund could muster neither the strength nor the will to lift a sword. Now he felt twenty years younger. Invincible. He had no men, but he had the finest pack of mastiffs in all of England. And the dog boy.

That night, Aurélie slept soundly in her clean, comfortable bed, the forbidden weight of Gabion across her feet and the velvet dress sizzling to nothing on the fire in the hall.

In the kennel sleeping lodge, Brind lay curled on the bracken with his head against Glaive's flank and the other hounds pressed around him. The dog boy was full of venison but still wide awake. He listened snugly to the drumming of the rain on the low roof, then raised his head to Glaive's ear.

'Plague healer,' he growled, then laughed out loud.